LEOPOLD VON SACHER-MASOCH

THE BLACK GONDOLA
AND OTHER STORIES

EDITED AND WITH AN INTRODUCTION BY

DANIEL CORRICK

THE BLACK GONDOLA
AND OTHER STORIES

LEOPOLD VON SACHER-MASOCH (1836-1895) was a novelist and social reformer whose fiction often explored the theme of feminine power and cruelty, as displayed in the corrupt high society of Imperial Vienna, as well as subjects from Slavic folklore and mythology. His principal work was the long and unfinished cycle of novellas which he published under the heading of *The Legacy of Cain*, the most famous of which was *Venus in Furs* (1869), an archetypical decadent work which became an important text of the Sexual Revolution and was an influence on artists as diverse as Franz Kafka and Lou Reed.

DANIEL CORRICK is an editor and literary historian with a specialist interest in nineteenth-century literature, especially the evolution of Gothicism and the Decadent movement. He has worked on a number of volumes including the collected fiction of Montague Summers, and unpublished works of Edgar Saltus and Edward Heron-Allen. In addition, he has edited several anthologies, including *Sorcery and Sanctity: A Homage to Arthur Machen* (Hieroglyphic Press, 2013), and *Drowning in Beauty: The Neo-Decadent Anthology* (Snuggly Books, 2018). He can be reached at: https://dccorick.com

for Afroditi

THIS IS A SNUGGLY BOOK

Introduction and Collection
Copyright © 2021 by Daniel Corrick.
All rights reserved.

ISBN: 978-1-64525-076-0

Contents

Introduction

MANY readers will only know the Austrian novelist and short story writer Leopold von Sacher-Masoch through the paraphilia to which he unwillingly lent his name. The only work of his widely known to English language readers is the novella *Venus in Furs*, which enjoys a niche reputation as the definitive work of masochistic erotica. Whilst it is treated more as a curiosity by literary historians, it exerted a formative influence on the developing fetish scene before and after the Sexual Revolution, inspiring much of the terminology and tropes associated with feminine dominance and master-slave relationships. Although that work deserves its place as a cultural artefact, other instance of Sacher-Masoch's fiction, especially his short stories, have more to offer both in terms of literary quality and fetishistic elements.

Sacher-Masoch's categorisation as a writer of erotica occurred retrospectively. During his lifetime, the Austrian was regarded as one of his nation's prime exponents of the Realist school, a documentarist of unvarnished human nature and an ethical progressive keen to highlight ongoing sociological conflicts in the hopes of encouraging reform. In his homeland his sympathetic stories of the Ruthenian minorities in the east of the Empire earned him epithet the "Galician Turgenev"; abroad, his support for female suffrage and tireless criticism of anti-Semitism won enthusiastic praise from liberally inclined figures including Émile Zola and Victor Hugo. So enthusiastic was the reception of his writings in France that he was awarded the Legion of Honour. It was the sensationalist autobiography of one of Sacher-Masoch's ex-wives and the coining of the term "masochism" by the sexologist Richard von Krafft-Ebing which affected his eventual conversion into a fetish icon.

Sacher-Masoch's formative influences both in terms of subject-matter and of the feminine symbolism he employs, were deeply rooted in the culture in which he grew up, that of early nineteenth-century Galicia, a multi-ethnic province of the Austrian Empire populated by the Jewish, Polish and Eastern Slavic or "Ruthenian" peoples. The son of an Austrian civic official and a Ruthenian noblewoman, his early education was undertaken by his mother's servants, in particular a nursemaid named Handzya, who entertained the young child with local fairy tales and folk songs. It is this woman Sacher-Maosch credits with shaping the trajectory of his psychological development, both in virtue of the passionate and forceful character she presented and of the world revealed by her stories. The influence of mythology and folk history on the author cannot be overestimated; they are probably of greater import than any individual quirk of upbringing or sexual make-up.

Slavic folklore abounded with instances of deadly women: sirens, witches, and evil spirits, often in implicitly sexualised scenarios; what's more, Death itself was often personified in the form of a woman, Morena or Mara, the folk survival of a pagan goddess whose symbolism we shall return to. More so than in other mythologies, the feminine as a Chthonic force incorporated not just fertility but also mortality and violence. Popular historical accounts were scarcely less sensationalist, the lives of the Tsars from Ivan the Terrible to Catherine the Great running crimson with cruelty and decadence, and the adventures of semi-legendary heroines such as Queen Esterka and Olga of Kiev presenting formidable, often ruthless women. Even the period contemporaneous with Sacher-Masoch's childhood was still marked by draconian power dynamics between the landed gentry and the peasant communities who worked the estates, many of whom were still treated as feudal property under the institute of serfdom. The cruelty of landowners, opulent and physically idle, to their strong but long-suffering and submissive serfs was a known trope treated with a degree of macabre relish—all the more so in the case of women where the vice was considered more "unnatural", given their assumed care-giver/mother role—as it supposedly demonstrated the stoical virtue of the peasant character.

The writer's aesthetic and perhaps psychological maturation constituted a synthesis between this supposedly atavistic eastern cultural heritage and the role of a "rationalistic" German intellectual as characterised by various scientific and revolutionary ideals. The years of his adolescence were marked by a tide of civil unrest as various ethnic factions struggled for greater autonomy from antiquated and overly bureaucratic Imperial governance. Fearful of revolution in Galicia, the family moved to Prague, only to witness street fighting and mass demonstrations in the Upheavals of 1848, an event which Sacher-Masoch would credit years later as first seeding his love of popular liberty. From 1854, Sacher-Masoch studied law and history at the University of Gratz, where, several years later, he obtained a teaching position lecturing on historical subjects. The dryness of an academic life held little appeal for him, however, and the learned articles soon gave way to short stories of Galician life after the manner of Russian novelists. The next decade saw him achieve fame with the novels *Don Juan of Kolomiya* and *The Divorced Woman*, both of which drew attention to the reduced legal rights of women in society, as well as painting a grim picture, influenced by Schopenhauer's notion of the Will to Live, of romantic love as underpinned by self-delusion and insatiable striving.

Sacher-Masoch's newfound fame encouraged him to embark on his most ambitious, though ultimately unfinished, project, a grand interlinking cycle entitled *The Legacy of Cain*, which was to be made up of six volumes of novellas, each dealing with one of the curses bequeathed to mankind by the Biblical pariah: *Love, Property, State, War, Work,* and *Death*. This work, clearly an attempt to compete with the social epics of Balzac and Zola, was left incomplete but contained some of his most famous stories, such as *Venus in Furs* and "Marcella", a version of which appears in this collection, both of which featured in *Love*.

The 1870s and early 1880s proved the high point of Sacher-Masoch's literary career with multiple novels and story collections appearing, as well as plaudits from famous writers abroad. Unfortunately, by then the public had grown aware of the link between the cruel women motif in his fiction and his own scandalous personal life; like the protagonist of his most well-known novel he engaged in contractual master-slave relationships with various women, most ill-fatedly with his once wife Aurora Rumelin, who wasted no time in gossiping about this with malicious zeal after the two had separated. This association with deviance eventually led to a cooling in critical enthusiasm, leaving Sacher-Masoch having to fight to prevent the (erroneous) label of pornographer from overshadowing his status as a man of letters. What the intelligentsia were happy to see portrayed as a sign of social ills they were unwilling to accept as a source of personal erotic pleasure. Although his remaining years were spent in comparative eclipse, Sacher-Masoch remained active in Austrian intellectual circles, organising various philanthropic ventures and publishing further criticisms of anti-Semitism along with the new threat of Prussian militarism. After suffering from a series of psychotic episodes which left both his mental and physical health impaired, his family placed him in a sanatorium, where he died soon after, in 1895.

Sacher-Masoch's stories of Ruthean "Little Russian" culture, those richest in symbolism and for which he was initially famous, are patterned after Ivan

Turgenev's *Sportsman's Notebook*, a portmanteau collection in which a narrator recounts anecdotes of the various peasants and small gentry he encounters over the course of the hunting season, the great Russian novelist's intent being to hint at the cruelty of serfdom. Sacher-Masoch employs similar devices, such as the dispassionate observer, the well-meaning urban visitor able to describe peasant life without vested interests; as an author he consciously plays down his own Ukrainian heritage in order to better present the "otherness" of these people to a Westernised German readership. Paradoxically, the vitality and mind-set of the supposedly primitive rural Slavs is often depicted as something Western revolutionary reform could learn from, as in "Marcella" and "The Harvest Home", in which the defiant, though moral, sensuality of the heroines presents a precursor to emancipated womanhood. As an author, Sacher-Masoch shows considerable skills, and intellectual self-awareness, in being able to put aside his own prejudices as a free-thinker and enter into the beliefs of the Ruthean countryman; as such, some of the stories incorporate folk symbolism, occult significations and, on occasion, obliquely supernatural phenomena, such as "The Letawitza", a fully-fledged weird story.

The most accomplished of the Galician stories is the short novella "Marcella". As has been mentioned, it was published alongside *Venus in Furs* and is best looked at in contrast to that novel. Sacher-Masoch's most famous work ends with the once masochistic protagonist, Severin, exerting a dominant role over a young servant girl, having learnt from his former slave relationship "that woman can only be slave or tyrant", in other words that erotic power dynamics mean that all relationships will reach an impasse where one partner has to establish control over the other. "Marcella", on the other hand, depicts the positive or constructive power of dominant femininity, wherein the primordial honesty of the titular heroine's peasant background renders her immune to the corrupting aspects of Westernised culture and allows her to engage with it on the same level as any man.

It is also the work wherein mythology and folk symbolism play the most prominent part. Marcella is as much the representation of a goddess as Wanda in *Venus in Furs*, albeit one far less familiar to the classicist tastes of Westernised Enlightenment readership. She is Morana, the queen of Death associated with the underworld and the darkness before the sprouting of new life. Throughout the story Sacher-Masoch makes implicit references to this figure, such as suggestions of witchcraft, spinning the weave of fates and the "cold" dark-haired maiden versus the inviting "solar" blonde conventionally associated with happiness. Like the Grim Reaper in Western iconography, this goddess is also depicted as wielding a scythe; with this in mind, the scene in the novella wherein the hero is struck by that implement has initiatory connotations—the suitor and his prideful old self must die in order to be proved worthy of the goddess. The sub-plot with the house snakes, once a real tradition in many parts of Central and Eastern Europe, also relates to this association, as stories of serpents and an envenomed kiss are associated with death goddess imagery in other Slavic cultures, such as that of Lithuania.

When it comes to stories of cosmopolitan life, Sacher-Masoch's emphasis is rather different: examples of virtue fade into the background and phenomena of erotic obsession, perversity, cruelty and abuse of power take centre stage. Many of these stories come from the two collections subtitled *The Messalinas of Vienna*, and deal with life in that capital from the perspective of a disenchanted and often amoral aristocratic class. In terms of subject matter they satisfy all the expectations the contemporary reader might have of Sacher-Masoch's fiction based on his reputation as the forefather of fetishism. "The Egoist" and "The Mountain of Venus" are classic femme-fatale stories featuring the Venus Dominatrix archetype, and the contracts in "The New Wife" and "A Cruel Test" parallel the contracts taken out with his various wives. The scenario laid out in "The Unknown Woman" corresponds to the early clinical idea of fetishism—that is, obsession with an unnatural object or situation without which an individual cannot experience physical desire.

In explaining these behaviours, Sacher-Masoch offers what has become a media cliché: that fetishism is the prerogative of the wealthy, since that class's freedom to indulge their appetites means they grow jaded with "healthy pleasures". In the opening paragraphs of "A Cruel Test", he gives his clearest account of its origins in women, stating explicitly that the slave or tyrant binary averred to in *Venus in Furs* arises from women shirking their natural roles of workers and mothers, and drifting into lives of frivolous experimentation for want of a more wholesome occupation. This depiction of virtuous working-class men exploited by decadent wealthy women parallels the abusive master/mistress and serf trope in the Ruthenian folk-rhetoric of his childhood. Ironically, for all his status as a freethinker and a revolutionary, Sacher-Masoch in fact ends up endorsing a variant on the Orthodox peasant view that cruelty in women arises from idleness, and is best avoided through worthy labour, albeit of the revolutionary rather than the Christian variety. Whilst this ultimately heteronormative stance on sexual relationships might strike some as disappointing, Sacher-Masoch still paints a sympathetic picture of assertive female sexuality and, in pieces such as "The Story of the Perpetual Student", at least acknowledges the possibility of a more mutually beneficial submissive relationship.

The dichotomy between Sacher-Masoch the social commentator and novelist and Sacher-Masoch the prophet of masochism is ultimately one based on changing historical perception rather than the content of his work. In addition to being one of the first European novelists to seriously explore an ancient but sociologically taboo form of eroticism, he also depicted it as part of a larger world-view incorporating mythology, cultural history and sociological critique. As more translations of his work become available, readers will see more of the richer substance of the artist beyond the shadows cast by *Venus in Furs*. His short fiction covers a greater range of erotic obsessions and possesses an incisive irony rivalling the best of the French *contes cruels*. The other novels explore the intellectual and personal tensions which shaped the nineteenth century. This volume will be the first but not the last selection from a strikingly individual writer whose talent has been too long eclipsed by his notoriety.

—Daniel Corrick

THE BLACK GONDOLA
AND OTHER STORIES

THE BLACK GONDOLA

SHE loved children with an overwhelming tenderness, and when she saw one with large, dark-brown eyes she always felt inclined to carry it off; her bosom heaved, she clasped her hands convulsively, and a painful smile hovered about her pale, compressed lips. Lia had never enjoyed the delights of maternity. Married to a man who was fond of her, who surrounded her with attentions and overwhelmed her with presents, she saw her youth fading away by the side of that strong, vigorous plant. She would gladly have been poor, to have begged her bread and to have slept upon straw, as long as she could have shared her bread and her straw with some light-haired rosy angel, who would have returned her caresses.

She was always thinking about this, and she would remain motionless for hours, with her eyes fixed on one spot in the room. She might have been taken for a statue, except that the colour of her cheeks and her flashing eyes betrayed a fixed idea and deep feeling in that beautiful breast.

She never betrayed herself before her husband; she laughed, she amused herself, she proposed the maddest excursions, said she was happy whilst her heart was full of weariness, the offspring of ennui, which soon turned to indifference. As she had thought, during the first years of her married life, that she should have a number of children, she had not wished for them.

"And yet they will come and only too many of them!" her friends said to her confidentially; but in the course of years this confident assurance grew less, and she began to indulge in fancies, and to suffer and to pray fervently. Yes, to pray, and never did a prayer rise from a more despairingly devout, or a more earnestly fervent soul. Then there came days of sweet expectation, of heavenly hopes, in which winter itself, with its monotonous white snow and gloomy sky, appeared beautiful to her: she went through the time when she first loved with its mysterious terrors and undefined longings, and at such times she shut herself up in the solitude of a remote country house, in order not to disturb her secret joy by the noise and bustle of a town, Then she re-appeared pale and agitated, and threw herself into the whirl of parties and balls, where she could pass her time without thinking, and lived on feverish excitement and false pleasures. And her husband was glad of it, for he wished to see her perfectly happy. And she was grateful to him for it, and she would gladly have loved him; but merely in the child she so longed for; within her heart she felt inexhaustible treasures of tenderness, which she would gladly have scattered broadcast, but not on that man who was her husband, without ever having been her lover.

One must love somebody, or something, and she
felt that necessity; but men appeared to her stupid,
and things in general intolerable, and after hunting
about for a long time, she fell in love with herself. And
then began a series of the most peculiar things; she
treated herself like a spoilt child, made herself presents of the most valuable jewels, remained alone for
hours in the small, pink drawing-room, intoxicated
with the various stupifying odours of tropical plants
and rare flowers; and she worshipped herself, her double, which she saw reflected in the large mirror. At
times she would give herself knowing or angry looks,
at others glowing kisses would expire on the cold glass
surface, without having touched the lips that were full
of desire, and then she clasped her arms together as if
embracing herself, so tightly that she left blue marks
on her arms. She whispered the sweetest, the most
loving words to herself in soft murmurs, and she started at the slightest noise and at every footstep. Then
would think of her schooldays, and of the months
which preceded her marriage, when she still thought
that she could be happy, or the succeeding years, in
which she reaped only disappointments. Then she
was seized with an intense longing to cry, and whilst
her heart really wept, her eyes remained dry, and her
sighs were turned into painful groans. She emerged
from the struggle with a pale face, with dull eyes,
with dark circles round them, and worn out in body;
she was afraid of herself. This searching for someone
else within herself, that doubling of herself, revealed
to her that she was even more solitary than formerly,
and that frightened her. Thirsting for love, she took

refuge in her husband, and always found in him the polite, obliging man, who was quite incapable of understanding her, or of alleviating her sufferings.

One night, in her despair, she had the horses put in and after a rapid drive, she found herself in the solitude of a villa, amongst the hills. She had been afraid of the town; after unspeakable temptations, and painful resistance she fled, in order not to yield, so as not to be vanquished by an enemy whom she despised, but who was dangerous, nevertheless.

The mountain air calmed her somewhat, whilst the thought that she had resisted, gave her courage; and she drove down to the extreme end of their property, to a villa on the shore of a lake, which was the fantastic offspring of an artist's mind. Her husband had various occupations; he was a barrister, a member of the Alpine Club, Provincial and Communal Councillor, a candidate for Parliament, and on that account was able to come and see her but seldom, and she rarely received her male, and, still more rarely, her female friends; obstinately remaining in her solitude, she was fond of comparing herself to a somnambulist, who walks on the edge of an abyss, and whom a breath of wind might dash over it.

She read, took walks, looked at the lake, the enchanting Laris, whose banks were covered with country houses, gardens, small woods and small landed properties; from time to time the whistle of a steamer, which was ploughing through the water, the sight of a white sail in the distance, or a passing boat, reminded her of that world which she feared, and which had not afforded her a single pleasure, hitherto.

And the bitter pleasure of sufficing to herself, traversed her heart again, like a snake that is released from its winter torpor. She was afraid of the darkness, and yet she remained leaning against the balustrade for a long time, and looked, absorbed in thought, into the dark water, which lay so quietly at her feet.

Here and there an indistinct light, almost lost in the distance, attracted her looks. "There," she, thought to herself, "is a poor boatman and a woman dressed in rags, who scarcely have enough to satisfy their hunger; but between them there is a child, a pretty, chubby-faced child, which makes them happy, whilst I . . ."

And for the remainder of the night she had no more rest; she felt tempted to tear the silk curtains and fine bedcovering to pieces, to take off her embroidered nightgear, and to throw all that unnecessary luxury into the lake. She put out the lamp, lighted it again, opened the window, as if somebody were waiting for her, and at last she threw herself onto the bed, dressed as she was, for she was thoroughly worn out; and even in her dreams, that terrible thought, followed her, that she was a young married woman with no one to love her, a married woman without children. She did not know why, but she expected somebody; it seemed to her as if she had been expecting him for a long time ever since her childhood, when she used to dream that she was the fair-haired daughter of a nobleman, and loved a handsome, dark page. That vision comforted her, and in the moments of her greatest solitude she spoke a thousand endearing words to him, and remonstrated with him for having kept her waiting so long.

Nobody would see him, he could love her in secret, no one would know it; the world is so wretched; it condemns you to suffer during your whole life, when a single word would be enough to turn sorrow into joy.

A night's rest, however, sufficed to drive away some of her fancies, and the next morning she carefully looked after her flowers and plants, for she wanted shade and scent, and so she planted them in shaded walks, near the steps, the railings and the windows. And so the days went on and she sat about and dozed because of the heat, whilst butterflies played around her and the sun caused a thousand flowers to unfold.

One morning a shot startled her from her peaceful frame of mind, and almost at the same moment a bleeding bird fell down at her feet, onto the edge of her dress.

With compressed lip, and flashing eyes and dilated nostrils she sprang up. She was very pale; and she made up her mind that she would question the insolent fellow who had done such a cruel thing, when, suddenly, a dog broke through the hedge and seized the booty, and immediately afterwards a young man appeared on the other side of the hedge, who appeared quite confused at the sight of her, and raising his hat very politely, tried to make some excuse, but the words stuck in his throat. She looked at him for a long time without moving; then her heart beat so, that she fell back onto her seat.

The young man came forward, and said with some embarrassment:

"I beg your pardon, Signora, I did not know that the villa was inhabited, and have been in the habit of shooting in the neighbourhood. Believe me that I am very much distressed . . . I wish I could punish myself for . . ."

Lia pointed to the gate at the other side of the walk, and with a deep bow he went, whilst she looked after him; when he got there, he turned round and bowed again.

She sat down and took up her book, but she could not read. She thought of him the whole day; in spite of her cursory glance, she had taken everything in; he was dark, had deep blue eyes, a pleasant voice, and very white hands. Then she began to compare him with her vision, the expected guest. He was not exactly the same; perhaps not quite so handsome, but more natural. She wished to see him again, and went and shut herself up in her drawing-room, and waited there feverishly all day. When it was getting dark, she went into the garden and watered a beautiful Night Viola, which she had in a large fancy vase on the terrace, as it was a plant that she was very fond of.

The cold water on her hands did her good; she bathed her forehead in it, and eagerly inhaled the moist breeze, which blew from the lake.

"He will not come again," she thought to herself; "I drove him away as if he had been a villain; I offended him, when he begged my pardon, so how could he come back?"

Then she feared lest he should come back; what could she say, or how could she receive him?

He was no stranger, she had been expecting him for a long time, she loved him. Almost at that moment she heard the sound of oars, and turning round, she saw the black gondola reflected in the lake, as it passed close to the garden walls of the villa. Then it went off again and then returned slowly and carefully, as if somebody were looking into the garden; and at last a man got out on the first steps which led from the lake into the garden, then came up higher and threw something into the pot of Violas.

She had remained motionless in the corner, but her heart was beating vehemently, and a thousand voices were exclaiming within her: "It is he! it is he . . ."

When he had disappeared she ran up to the flower pot and found a letter in it. When she touched it, it went through her as if she had been bitten by a serpent; her gentle mother's image rose before her eyes, and made her hesitate for an instant, but the feeling was not strong enough to restrain her. When she had got into the house, she read it over and over again; he also had been looking for a woman who corresponded to his dreams, and now he blessed the accident, which had brought her to him; he was too obscure to hope for love; but he begged for a meeting, that she might learn to know him. He also begged for secrecy for her own sake, as he did not wish to compromise her, but he ventured to hope for her forgiveness.

They were the sort of phrases that one reads so frequently, but Lia discovered a whole future of devotion and of love in them. And whilst she was indulging in visions for the future, she forgot the past and even the present, and replied by a long letter, much moved, and with tears in her eyes, and told him her troubles, of her longing for love, of her hopes, and concluded by throwing herself into his arms.

When she had finished, she raised her head; it felt so heavy, and the bronze satyr who carried the lamp was laughing with pleasure. The plants and flowers exhaled intoxicating odours, and little imps with strange shadows crept out of the embroidered window curtains.

She read what she had written over again; it seemed to her much too high-flown, and so she tore it up, and wrote on a fresh sheet of paper the simple words:

"I forgive you!"

And worn out and excited she threw herself onto her bed.

After that, the black gondola came every evening, and every evening the fair-haired woman extended her small white hand to the gondolier, to be kissed. She did not allow him anything more, but she let him hope that one day perhaps . . .

And one day her husband arrived in much excitement; they must prepare for the grand regatta on the lake; some of the Ministers were coming, and the whole Italian and foreign Press would speak about them; there was no time to be lost so Lia shrugged her shoulders, and let him have his way. And certainly their villa with its grandeurs, its thickets and long walks down into the lake, outdid all others on the evening of the fête, and the owner's eyes glistened with satisfaction.

The lake wore a wonderfully phantastic appearance; its shores and surface glowed in the most variegated flames; on the hills there were huge bon-fires, and rockets were sent up; the villas displayed fireworks, and the country houses stood out brightly from the dark background.

Steamers with festoons of coloured lamps, rafts with bands of singers, canoes and hundreds of boats darted about in all directions, whilst the mountains re-echoed with the noise of shots. It was an orgy of light, a fable of voices, a crowd of people, but everything went on as harmoniously as a pleasant dream.

Lia retired early, nearly worn out; she did not wish to be disturbed, and her husband was quite capable of doing the honours of the house alone. But when the fête was at its height, she went into the garden through a private door, walked along the hedges on tiptoe, and as far as the steps which led up to the park. The black gondola was lying there perfectly motionless; it received her hospitably and darted off like an arrow, only to be lost in the darkness.

When she came home again, the lights were already out, the lake was peacefully slumbering, and her husband, who was delighted because he had shaken hands with two Ministers, already saw himself a Deputy, in his dreams. But Lia, very pale, guilty and happy, went to sleep with a smile on her face, and dreamt of the black gondola, and of a fair baby.

THE EGOIST

ON a dull winter morning, Frederick Brieg, the painter, was standing in front of his easel in his room, for the small, poorly furnished, apartment did not deserve the name of studio, and was laying the ground colours on to the canvas. Although he looked rather out of temper, and in spite of his neglected dress, nobody could deny that he was a handsome man. He was tall, and had a striking and interesting face; he wore a full black beard, though his hair was beginning to get thin, but his eyes had still the brightness of youth, and in his looks there was that indescribable something that forcibly impresses men, and sends women into raptures.

There was a knock at the door.—"Come in!"— And a girl, who was closely veiled and wrapped in a cloth cloak, came in and went up to the painter. "What can I do for you?" Brieg said, without interrupting his work.

"Are you Herr Brieg, the painter?" the girl asked, rather shyly.

"Certainly, and may I ask what you want?"

"You require a model, I think," the girl said, in a low voice.

Brieg now looked at her more closely, but he did not succeed, in making out either the lines of her face nor of her figure.

"And you wish? . . ." he asked her at last.

"I have made up my mind," the girl replied. "My father lately met with an accident at the factory where he works, and I must do something to procure money for my parents, otherwise, we should all have to commit suicide, and it is surely better for me to become a painter's model and remain virtuous than to sacrifice my honour. I am told that models are well paid."

"Certainly."—And the painter mentioned his terms.

"But I have also some request to make," the girl said. "In the first place, you must not introduce my face into your picture, and next, I must have some money on the spot."

"I agree to them," the painter replied; "but as you must have heard that I require a model for a Venus, I must first of all see whether you are suitable."—The girl threw off her cloak and veil, and now stood before the painter with her thick, dark hair twisted into a simple knot, which set off her figure perfectly, and the painter stepped back in astonishment at her extraordinary beauty.

"Are you satisfied?" the girl began.

"Yes, but I shall be the most unhappy of painters, if you will not allow me to paint your face also," Brieg exclaimed. "You are wonderfully beautiful, and it would be a sin . . ."

The model shook her head.

"I have a proposal to make to you," Brieg continued; "I will paint another Venus's head to your body, and your head to another body."

"I have nothing to say against that," the girl said. "And when do you want to begin?"

"Immediately."—And the painter got his easel ready with strange haste.

"Immediately?" the girl repeated in terror, whilst a deep blush covered her beautiful face.

"I must beg you to allow me to," the painter replied, with a bow. Then he locked the door.

She remained standing for a moment as if she were petrified, and then she began to undress impetuously, and soon she stood before the painter, as beautiful as Venus rising from the foam of the sea, covering her face with her hands, and weeping bitterly.

"Good heavens!" the painter exclaimed, "had I anticipated this, I would never have allowed . . ."

"Yes, it must be done," the girl said "so put me in the position you require, and begin to paint."

Brieg scarcely ventured to touch his model, but he hastily drew an outline of his picture, and gave it to the girl, saying: "This is how I want you to stand, if you please."

She looked at the piece of paper for a long time, and then suddenly put herself in the attitude which the painter's fancy had prescribed for her, but which exceeded the picture which Brieg had imagined to himself so greatly in pureness of out-line and beauty, that Brieg was obliged to put great restraint on himself, so as not to give a shout of joy, and he began to draw with the charcoal, and at the end of half an hour he said: "That is enough for today."

Then he turned away to the window, until the girl was dressed, who took the money that he gave her, without speaking, and then quickly left the room, but she returned the next day, and on every succeeding day, and the relations between them became peculiar.

Neither of them spoke a word, but every time that he took his eyes off her, she looked at the handsome gifted painter, who treated her with so much respect, with a half shy, half tender glance, but when he devoured her with his ardent gaze, she looked modestly and chastely on to the ground, until at last the moment came, when the painter threw aside brush and palette, and threw himself down at his model's feet.

"What are you doing?" the girl stammered.

"Forgive me, but I am beside myself," Brieg exclaimed. "I am no longer master of myself; I love you; will you become my wife?"

The poor girl covered her face with her hands, and was silent, whilst the painter rose and went back to his easel. When he had done, he went to the window, as usual, and for some time nothing was heard in the room except the rustling of a woman's clothes, which the painter listened to with a sensation which he had never experienced before. A nameless dread seized him, lest he should lose her altogether and forever. But the rustling came nearer, and a hand was laid gently on his shoulder.

"Do you really love me?" the beautiful girl began shyly.

"I do not know how I shall manage to live without you any longer," the painter replied. "Does that satisfy you?"

"Then take me," she said, hesitatingly.

"You will . . . you do not hate me?" he almost shouted.

"I have loved you from the first moment," the girl whispered through her tears. "Can you now guess what I have endured?"

"I have also been obliged to suffer nameless torments," the painter cried; "but now everything has come right, and nothing in the world shall separate us."

The girl's name was Theresa Merk and she was the child of poor people, but she was an honest, respectable girl, and by no means uneducated, and Brieg fully made up his mind to marry her as soon as he had made a position for himself. They formed golden plans for the future together, and who knows whether these would not have been fulfilled, if the girl had not given herself up to her lover too soon, when she was his altogether, yet his love was ambitious, and above all things, egoistical.

He had exhibited the two pictures, for which his mistress had served him as his model, and expected unusual results from them; his disillusion, therefore, was all the more bitter, when they neither obtained the approbation of the critics nor purchasers.

"I do not succeed, because I have no influence," he said to Theresa, who felt uneasy at his dark looks. "What is the good of talent, or even of genius, without the favour of influential people, and a female Mæcenas, in whose eyes the athletic limbs of the artist have found favour, is even in a position to make him able to dispense with talent altogether." He laughed bitterly, and the poor girl, who loved him with all her heart, was now daily obliged to suffer more and more, on account of his shipwrecked hopes. He had many cares, and was often obliged to eat dry bread. Then his temper became something terrible, and all her love and devotion could not smooth his brow. But one day as he was loitering aimlessly about the streets, he accidentally attracted the notice of a lady of rank, as she was driving by. She was the countess Leontine Holnstein, one of the empress's ladies in waiting, a thorough woman of the world, without a heart, and perhaps without passions, a woman who only measured love by her whims and her taste. She had just dismissed one of her adorers, and was feeling bored and Brieg struck her. She made inquiries about him, and the next day a scented note invited him to her mansion.

The painter went immediately, and he found a voluptuous blonde of nearly forty, who, however, still looked decidedly desirable, and who succeeded in captivating him, in the first half-hour, in the meshes of an animated conversation, and it was settled that Brieg was to paint the countess. She herself chose the dress, which was of black velvet, and extremely low, so as to show her bosom in all its beauty. Brieg went to the house to paint her, but the picture made very slow progress, as she preferred to chat and flirt with the interesting painter.

Once she surprised him in his studio, and found Theresa there. The countess stared at the girl through her double eye-glasses, turned up her nose, and gave the painter a significant look. Whereupon Brieg gave his mistress a sign to leave the room, which she reluctantly obeyed.

"Who is that person?" she asked.

"A poor girl who acts as my model," the painter replied.

"Well, I think a man of your genius has no necessity for looking for his models amongst the scum of the people," the countess replied. "What would you say if I were willing to become your Fornarina?"

The painter stared at her in surprise, and she continued: "You interest me, and I will patronise you. But you must school your talent according to the classical models, and I propose that you go to Italy with me."

"With you? But then you will have to love me; can you do that?"

The next moment the painter was lying at her feet, and that experienced woman of the world gave a pleased smile, and almost immediately after she had left him Theresa returned to the studio. She overwhelmed him with reproaches, but he interrupted her coldly

"I shall never get on as things are now," he said, with perfect self-possession. "You cannot expect me to die of hunger for your sake, when celebrity and fortune are within my grasp. I am going to Italy with the countess, and we must part."

"Consider what you are doing," Theresa, who was nearly desperate, said.

"I have already thought it over carefully."

"Frederick, I love you, but if you are a villain, as you seem to be—then—I shall not rest until I have been revenged on you," the unhappy girl cried.

Brieg smiled carelessly, and giving him a last look, in which there was as much love as hatred, she rushed out of the room.

A year later, Frederick Brieg, the favourite of the Countess Holnstein, and of the Court, was Director of the Royal Picture Gallery, all the upper classes had their portraits painted by him, and the Prince gave him permission to paint his mistress, the celebrated singer, Flora Herisson. Brieg did not fail to be at the house of the influential beauty, at the appointed time, who was lying on a couch, in a pink satin dressing-gown, lined with ermine. She laughed as he came into the room, but it was a laugh which made the painter shiver.

"Don't you know me again?" a well-known voice said, and he began to tremble all over, for it was Theresa. He tried to make excuses for the way in which he had treated her, but she cut him short.

"You were commanded to come here to paint my portrait," she said, haughtily and contemptuously. "Let us stick to the matter in question."

He painted her, and whilst the work was in prog-ress, repentance and passion arose in his heart, at the sight of that woman, who was as lovely as she was seductive, until at last, he was seized by the frenzy of loves, and he threw himself at her feet; she, however, only laughed, and ordered him to go on painting.

"Theresa," he said, almost weeping, "this moment I feel, that I love you, and you only; do not drive me from you, for I cannot live without you."

"You lie!"

"I am not lying!"

"Really? Then, I am avenged," she exclaimed with devilish glee, "for I do not love you; I love the Prince, so what is the love of a poor painter to me?" And with these words she left the room.

Brieg felt annihilated: and from that time every-thing went wrong with him; he fell into disgrace with the Prince, and in spite of the Countess' intercession, he was dismissed from his post. Theresa kept her word; she had her revenge. Disappointed ambition, humiliation and despised love accelerated a malady, the germs of which had been sown by the favours of the amorous Countess. She, however, appeared to pity her adorer, who was destined for an early death; she took him to Nice with her, where she left him, and went to Naples with a handsome Italian Marquess, "for it would affect her nerves too much to see him die," she said, and so he was left alone at that supreme hour, when he had to face death. But he did not remain alone, for he was aroused from his hopeless brooding by the appearance of a beautiful woman, in a red velvet cloak, which was worthy of a queen: it was Theresa.

"You here—you," he groaned, "have you at last taken pity on me?"

"No," she replied, in cold, heartless accents; "it is hatred that brings me hither; I want to see you die, so be quick about it, for the Prince, my husband, is waiting down below in his carriage."

"I am not going to die yet," the unhappy painter managed to say: "I will not die."

The lovely woman stood at the foot of his bed and laughed, and whilst she was laughing, he expired.

When she leant over him; she was appeased, and great tears rolled down her cheeks, and fell on to the face of the dead man.

THE DRUNKARD

THE north wind was blowing fiercely, driving great banks of heavy, black, wintry clouds across the sky, from which furious showers descended, as they passed overhead, whilst the sea raged, and beat against the shore in huge waves, which dashed against the beach with a roar like artillery. They came on slowly, one after the other, mountain-high, scattering the white foam from their crests in the air, like the froth from some monstrous, wild animal.

The storm whistled and howled through the little valley, and tore the tiles off the roofs, broke the shutters, blew down the chimneys, and almost knocking over the foot passengers in the streets, who could only walk by holding on to the walls, whilst if children had been out in it, they would have been whirled up like leaves, and carried over the houses.

The fishing boats had been drawn up high above the beach, as the sea would sweep it at high tide, whilst some sailors, crouching behind the vessels which were lying on their sides, watched the tempest of the sky and seas, and then by degrees they went away, for night was falling over the scene, and wrapping the mad ocean, and all the turmoil of the infuriated elements in darkness.

Two men, however, remained, with their hands in their pockets, and bending beneath the sudden squalls. They had pulled their woollen caps down to their eyes, and were two tall, Normandy fishermen, with rough, straggling beards, their skin tanned and weather-beaten, and with blue eyes with a black speck in the middle, those piercing sailors' eyes, which can see to the verge of the horizon, like a bird of prey.

One of them said:

"Come along, Jeremiah; we will pass our time at dominoes; I will pay."

The other hesitated, tempted by the game and the brandy, but knowing that he should get drunk again if he went into Paurnelle's, and restrained also by the thought of his wife, who was all by herself in their cottage, and he replied:

"One might think that you had made a bet to make me drunk every night. I say, what good does it do you, as you always pay?"

And he laughed at the idea of all that brandy he had drunk at another man's expense, whilst his companion, Mathurin, kept on pulling him by the arm.

"Come along, Jeremiah. It is not the evening to go home without anything warm in one's stomach. What are you afraid of? Do you think your wife will forget to warm your bed?"

But Jeremiah replied:

"I could not find the door the other evening . . . they had to fish me out of the brook that runs in front of our house! And he laughed again at the recollection of his drunken mishap, and then went slowly towards Paurnelle's Café, where the lights shone brightly through the windows, and he went in, dragged by Mathurin and driven through the wind, quite incapable of resisting their combined forces.

The lower room was full of sailors, of smoke and noise, for all the men in their woollen clothes and their arms resting on the table were shouting to make themselves heard. The more drinkers that came in, the more necessary it was to shout, amidst the confusion of voices, and of the dominoes rattling on the marble tables, to increase the din.

Jeremiah and Mathurin went and sat down in a corner and begun their game, whilst the small glasses of brandy disappeared down their capacious throats, and then they played some more games and had more brandy. Mathurin kept on pouring it out and winking at the landlord, a fat man with a face as red as fire, and who laughed continually as he had some capital joke in his head, and Jeremiah swallowed the brandy, wagged his head and gave vent to laughter which sounded like the roaring of some wild beast, whilst he looked at his companion in a stupid and satisfied manner.

All the customers left, and every time that one of them opened the outer door to leave, a gust of wind came into the Café, and blew about the heavy cloud of tobacco smoke, made the lamps swing backwards and forwards and nearly blew them out. Occasionally was heard the deep thunder of a wave lashing against the beach and the roaming of the squall.

Jeremiah sat there like a drunken man does, with his collar unbuttoned, and with one leg stretched out, and one arm dangling by his side, whilst with the other hand he held his dominoes. They were alone now with the landlord, who had come and was watching them, much interested in their game, and he asked:

"Well, Jeremiah, how is your inside? Have you refreshed it, by dint of watering it?"

And he stammered: "The more that goes into it, the drier it gets, inside there."

The landlord looked at Mathurin cunningly, and said: "What about your brother, Mathurin? Where is he now?"

The sailor laughed silently, and replied: "He is in the warm; do not distress yourself."

And they both looked at Jeremiah who triumphantly put down the double sixes and said: "There you are!"

When they had finished their game, the landlord said: "Well, you know I am off to bed. I will leave you a lamp and another bottle; there is a franc's worth of brandy in it. Lock the door from the outside, Mathurin, and push the key under the shutter, like you did the other night," to which Mathurin replied: "All right!" and the landlord shook hands with them, and left them and went slowly up the wooden stairs. For some minutes his heavy steps resounded through the house, and then a loud creaking announced that he had gone to bed. The two men went on playing, and from time to and time a wilder gust than usual shook the door and made the walls tremble, and the two drinkers raised their eyes as if someone were about to come in. Then Mathurin took up the bottle and filled Jeremiah's glass, and at that moment the clock over the counter struck twelve, and Mathurin got up immediately, like a sailor whose watch is over, and said:

"Come, Jeremiah, we must be off."

He, however, found it more difficult to move, and balanced himself, by resting his hands on the table; then he went to the door and opened it, whilst his friend put out the lamp, and when they were in the street, Mathurin locked the door, and said: "Well, goodnight until tomorrow."

Jeremiah went on for three paces, then staggered, stretched out his hands, which touched the wall, so that he could keep himself up, and set off to try and walk again. Now and then, a puff of wind in the narrow street would send him off running for a few yards, but as soon as its violence was over, he stopped altogether, as he had lost his propeller, and again he began to vacillate on his capricious, drunkard's legs. However, he went instinctively towards his house, like birds fly to their nest, and at last he recognized his door and began to fumble at it, in order to find the lock and insert the key, but he could not find the key-hole, and began to swear in a low voice, then he hammered at the door with his fist, and called to his wife to come and let him in:

"Mélina! Here! Mélina!"

He was leaning against the door, so that he might not fall down, when it gave way and flew open, and Jeremiah, having lost his support, went into his house head first, and fell on his nose in the middle of the passage, and whilst lying there, he felt something heavy step over him and flee away into the night.

He did not move, as he was flurried with fear, in terror of the devil, of ghosts and of all the mysterious creatures of darkness, and he waited for a long time, without venturing to move, but when he saw that all was still and nothing stirring, he recovered a gleam of reason, of the dull, confused reason of a drunken man, and he sat down quietly. He waited for some time longer, and then getting a little braver he called out: "Mélina!" But still his wife did not reply, and then suddenly a suspicion crossed his clouded brain, an undecided, vague suspicion. He did not move, but remained where he was, sitting on the ground in the dark, trying to collect his thoughts, which were as undecided and wavering as his legs, and again he asked her:

"Tell me who it was, Mélina? Tell me who it was and I will not do anything to you."

He waited, but got no reply, and then he began to reason with himself in a loud voice: "He gave me all that liquor in order that I should not go home; I am dreadfully drunk!" And then he continued: "Tell me who it was Mélina, or I shall do you some mischief."

After waiting for some time longer, he continued, with the slow and obstinate logic of a drunken man:

"He kept me at that ne'er do well Paurnelle's, and the other evenings as well, so that I would not go home. It is an accomplice of his. Ah! the brute!"

He knelt down slowly; he was seized with furious rage, which added to the fermentation of the drink he had taken, and he repeated:

"Tell me who it was, Mélina, or I shall strike, I tell you!"

Then he stood up again, shaking with rage, as if the alcohol which he had in his body had taken fire in his veins. He took a step forward, knocked up against a chair, took it up and went forward, knocked up against the bed, touched it and felt the warm body of his wife in it, and mad with rage, he growled:

"Oh! So you were here, you dirty slut, and did not give me any answer."

And lifting up the chair which he was holding in his strong, sailor's hands, he brought it down in front of him in all the exasperation of his rage, and a cry issued from the bed, a heartrending, terrible cry, and then he began to beat away, like a thresher in a barn, and soon all was still. The chair was in pieces, but one of the legs remained in his hand, and be kept on beating on the bed, and panting for breath, and then stopped suddenly but and asked:

"Will you tell we now who it was?" but Mélina did not reply, and he, worn out with fatigue and by his own violence, stretched himself out on the ground and went to sleep, and in the morning a neighbour, seeing the door open, went in. He found Jeremiah snoring on the ground, on which the remains of the chair were lying, and the dead, battered body of the woman in the bed.

ADAM AND EVIL

ON the present occasion, we shall give our hero, and certainly not without reason, the name of the first man, for it is a story of a forfeited Paradise, that we are going to relate.

The scene is laid in a German town, which is fortunate enough to possess a Court with a Monarch, Chamberlains, ladies-in-waiting, Court scullions and a Court theatre, where scullions go into the gallery, the ladies and the Chamberlains into the pit, but their majesties into the royal box, which is hung in red velvet.

Adam was a tenor singer at this Court theatre, and Eve a young ballet girl; she was not his wife, however. This is certainly contrary to the Bible, but such exceptions occur frequently nowadays both in the Old and New Testament, that the rule will very soon become the exception. In spite of this, however, Adam had a lawful wife, whom he was said to have married for her money, and certainly nobody could ever discover any bodily advantages in her.

In addition to this, she was very jealous, like all ugly women who have good-looking husbands invariably are, and Adam was a handsome man in the acceptation of the term, as even old Countess Emmeline Grütz-Knoll-Bombenkessel, the widow of the celebrated general of that name, and she was a lady who knew the male sex from Prince down to groom, thoroughly, and who was, therefore, quite competent to give an opinion.

Adam was tall, but at the same time as slim and elastic as the Apollo of the Belvedere; dark curls surrounded his sunburnt beardless face, in which two black eyes flashed like stars; his small mouth, with its splendid, white teeth immediate aroused the idea of kisses in every woman, and this was also the case with fair-haired Eve, for our Eve of the ballet was naturally fair-haired, and contrasts always attract each other.

She was fair, but fair like the Venetians painted fair women; for it is well known that in Venice the ladies used to bleach their hair by a very original and extensive system of manipulation, on the flat roofs of their palaces, which thus retained some gleam of the red sun. And were not Lucretia Borgia and Mary Stuart, those two great sinners in genuine ermine, both light-haired? And then Eve, like that amiable Papal poisoner, had black, dreamy eyes with her light hair.

She first met Adam at the rehearsals at the Court theatre very frequently, for those Operas in which the ballet is not introduced in order to add to the attraction of the music are very rare, and the attractive diabolical girl immediately took the handsome singer's fancy, and soon they came to a thorough understanding; even before they had exchanged a word.

She used to stand in the wings when he sang and never took her eyes off him, and when she was dancing, he did the same thing, and at last they spoke together for the first time in the mysterious half light of the slips.

The stage has two quite different, almost opposite aspects. In the evening, when a performance is going on, hundreds of gas-jets are burning, which shed a glare of light into every corner. Then there is no place for concealment behind the footlights, then nothing can be hidden, but it is very different in the day, during rehearsals, when the whole building is in semi-darkness, and it was in those silent, twilight hours that the love of the tenor singer, and of the light-haired ballet girl began, grew and found expression, until at last, one evening when he was not going to sing, and knew that she was at home, he mounted the four steep flights of stairs.

That little attic of hers then became a Paradise. The poor and pretty girl loved the renowned singer, with whom so many countesses and baronesses flirted from their boxes, and to whom so many highly-born Messalina's sent perfumed notes, which he did not answer, with all the ardour of her young heart, and he often looked forward for a whole week to the evening which he should spend in her company; and when her mother, whose eyes sparkled with pride as soon as he came in, had closed the door behind him, all the petty details and cares of every day life, which as a rule embitter our existence more than real sorrow or actual pain, were left on the other side of the threshold.

But the ballet girl with the Borgia hair, was not only beautiful and in love with him but also very unselfish, whilst the wife of the tenor sat so suspiciously over her money bags, and watched her husband's expenditures so closely, that he was hardly able to bestow any little attentions upon her, but she never accepted anything from him without reluctance, and blushed deeply whenever he made her a present, and at last, when he had secretly scraped together crown after crown, and made her a present of a bracelet at Christmas, she threw it angrily at his feet, and burst into tears, and thus it came about, that our Adam began to bestow favour on her mother, in various ways.

Amongst other things, he regularly brought her a ticket for a reserved seat at the theatre for those evenings when he sang. He got it at the box-office himself, and another one for his wife.

By an unfortunate accident, however, he one day got two seats next to each other, and without looking at the numbers, he unsuspectingly gave one to the mother of his Eve and the other to his wife, so that the two ladies sat together during the performance.

Mamma Eve, who was a thoroughly good-natured Viennese woman, who was quite incapable of sitting in a theatre without entering into conversation with her neighbour, turned to his wife, whom she did not know, at the close of an act, in which he had sung magnificently and had been greatly applauded, and said with a sigh of satisfaction:

"What a splendid voice, Adam has; do you not think so?"

"I am really not justified in giving an opinion . . ."

"Why not," Mamma Eve said, interrupting her, "I am not musical either, but then we all of us have our feelings; in fact, mine are too easily excited, and then Adam is such a charming fellow, off the stage as well, I can tell you; especially off the stage, indeed; I am quite carried away merely when I see him, and so you may think how it is when I hear him sing."

"So you know him?" his wife said, whose suspicions were aroused.

"Of course I know him," the good-tempered woman replied, "and very intimately too."

"Intimately?"

"Yes, I see him and talk with him nearly every day," the chatty old woman continued. "He is a dear fellow, I tell you."

"Indeed!" his wife said, incredulously.

"Do you know," Mamma Eve said in a confidential whisper, after she had looked round carefully, to see that nobody was listening, "there is something between him and my daughter."

The singer's wife certainly grew pale, but she did not lose her composure, for she wished to find out all about the matter.

"What is your daughter?" she asked politely, and even managing to smile as she said it.

"She is a ballet girl."

"And what is her name?"

Without hesitation Mamma Eve told her name, and the singer's wife continued her examination and the old woman went on chattering, until the curtain fell for the last time, and she told her when they got home, what charming lady sat next to her at the theatre, who was also enthusiastic about her Adam.

The next morning, however, he came to see his fair-haired Eve, and did not seem at all pleased with her mother's diplomatic skill. His wife had had a terrible scene with him, and threatened him with a judicial separation; and whilst he was giving vent to his ill-temper to his beloved, her mother, who was so enthusiastic about him, came in.

"I am very glad to see you, Mr. Adam."

"Well, I am not at all glad to see you today, Mamma Eve," the tenor who was terribly exasperated, replied.

"I must really beg . . ."

"You have played me a pretty trick," Adam continued. "She has raised up hell against me; do you know who was sitting next to you in the theatre last night?"

"No, I do not."

"The lady with whom you were talking to with such animation, and to whom you so kindly gave a detailed account of the terms on which I am with your daughter . . ."

"I have not the honour . . ."

"That lady was my wife."

"Good heavens! The saints protect us," Mamma Eve exclaimed. "And I have just remembered that the lady who was sitting next to me at the Opera yesterday, if she really is your wife, is looking out for you downstairs."

"Where?"

"Just outside our house," the Mamma replied.

"She is pacing up and down like a sentry. I knew her again immediately, but she did not see me, although she has glasses on."

"She is quite capable of coming upstairs," Adam exclaimed.

"We are lost," the pretty ballet girl cried, and broke out into hysterical sobs; at last, however, all of them with the exception of the dog, on whose paws the tenor singer had trodden in his excitement, recovered their composure, and consulted together how they could avoid a catastrophe. More than one plan was considered, and given up as impracticable, until at last, the harmless cause of the mischief, Mamma Eve, discovered the way of safety and salvation; and her proposal, which was applauded by the lovers, was immediately put into execution.

Adam put on a dress with a long train belonging to his sweetheart, with a large waterproof cloak over it, fastened by a chignon on his head, and bonnet and thick veil, and in ten minutes he stood as a tall, majestic woman in the ballet girl's little room. Mamma Eve put on a hood, so that she might not be recognized, and then she gave her arm to the culprit and led him downstairs and out of the house, and when his wife saw two women coming out, she saw nothing suspicious or striking in it.

They soon found a cab, and told the driver to take them to a certain street as quickly as possible. There they got out, and in the first dark entry they came to the tenor singer threw off his wraps, and Mamma Eve quickly returned home with them.

That time the lovers were saved, but for the future the tenor's jealous wife did not allow him to go out alone and even accompanied him to rehearsals, or when he went to a *café* until at last she became the cherub with the fiery sword, which drove Adam and Eve out of their Paradise—forever.

People say that Adam looked very cross for some time, but Eve, after she had mourned for him in a becoming fashion for a month or so, consoled herself with a lieutenant of curassiers, who was six foot tall.

THE GRAVE-DIGGER'S DAUGHTER

A RATTLE of musketry came from the direction
of the village. The old grave-digger, Boloski,
wakened by the noise, sat up on his miserable pallet,
listened a moment to the sharp, quick reports then
called aloud: "Milena! Milena!"

"Coming, father, coming!" she answered, and already the little naked feet showed themselves upon
the rungs of the ladder which led from the loft.

"Did you hear them, Milena?" he cried; "the
sounds of the gun shots? They are fighting in the
village." A violent attack of coughing interrupted his
words, and another rattling volley.

Milena had descended just as she quitted her
couch of straw,—a young girl, tall and vigorous, and
scantily draped in a brief chemise. She had thrown
about her shoulders a short pelisse of sheepskin, but
her Amazon hips showed themselves firm and beautiful under their light covering, and her virginal breasts
appeared an instant, white as polished marble, against
the black fur.

"It is true, then!" she said, leaping the last steps; "it
has come at last?"

"What, my child?" demanded the sick one.

"The Revolution has broken out tonight, which has been expected so long."

"Yes, and a great misfortune it is too," mumbled Boloski, and he crouched again upon his couch. Milena, meanwhile, hurriedly arrayed herself in a wadded petticoat and her father's long boots. Binding a scarlet handkerchief about her abundant locks, she went out to learn what was passing.

The cemetery was situated upon a hill, surrounded by a low earthen wall, with the hut of the grave-digger standing at its gate. It was an excellent post of observation, yet Milena did not stop there, but passed on into the darkness, beneath the bare branches of the willows, upon which the ravens were already croaking, and with a single careless glance upon the files of tombs, with their leaning crosses. Everything was mournful and desolate, everything covered by the melancholy shroud of winter. She herself walked in snow so deep and thick that it mounted almost to her knees. The cold was terrible: the frozen breath of the night whipped and stung the skin like red-hot needles, but Milena only rubbed her face with a handful of snow and buttoned her pelisse closer.

Below, in the heart of the valley, the village had delivered itself up to the strife and bloodshed, yet here upon the sacred ground all was peace. A large cross rose in the middle of the enclosure, to which was attached the figure of the dying Saviour; icicles pendant from the thorns which covered his crown and from the nails which pierced his hands and feet.

Milena listened intently; not a murmur for the moment broke the stillness. She stopped and gazed up at the heavens, the vast blue vault which seemed to her a satin canopy, retained in place by the golden nails which sparkled and scintillated above her, while beyond, on the other side of the forest, rose the red disc of the rising moon.

All at once a gliding, crouching form passed her like a flash, a pair of glowing eyeballs glared into her own.

"A wolf!" she murmured, and, with an energetic movement, wherein shone all the savage strength of this child of nature, she seized a stone from the neighbouring wall and threw herself forward. A low howl responded to the stroke of her arm, and the hungry beast was gone as it had come—a shadow—through those files of tombs and spectral crosses.

A fresh crash of musketry sounded in the distance, another and still another. Milena traversed at a run the slope of the road which led to the village, and, at the beginning of the first houses, met a neighbour and a wounded man, the wife, whom she knew well, supporting her husband, whose blood dyed the snow at every step.

"What is the matter?" demanded Milena.

"The peasants of our village," replied the man, "and of Mikonloff are struggling with the insurgents down by the *café* and the little wood. All goes well, however; the scythes are sharp and do their mowing; the heads fall like grain!"

"So!" said Milena; and she aided the peasant woman to place her husband in his bed and to bind his wounds. Then she retraced her steps to tranquillise her father.

An hour later a loud knocking sounded upon the gate of the cemetery.

"See what it is, Milena," said the grave-digger again; and Milena, obeying the command, opened the wicket obstructed by frost, to find before it a row of sledges encompassed by horsemen, the barrels of their muskets and the blades of their sickles sparkling in the rays of the moon.

"Come, open the gate, old mole!" shouted a voice from the crowd; "Open the gate and open quickly. We bring you a score of distinguished guests!"

"But I want no guests," replied Boloski from the interior. "I am ill, as you know well, I dare not go out in a night like this."

"Ill or no," cried the voice again, "the work must be done."

"Well bury them yourself, then."

"We cannot; we have not the time."

"In that case," said Milena, brusquely, shutting the wicket end to the discussion, "'tis I who shall bury them for you." And she went out to open the gate for the four loaded sledges, bearing the dead bodies of the insurgents, and too the conquerors, armed with their bloody sickles and gleaming scythes.

"Throw them there upon the snow," said she to the mayor of the village, who greeted her as she appeared with a friendly nod; "I'll start the business for you at the rising of the sun."

"No," said the Mayor, "that would not be Christian; the wolves and ravens are already waiting to do their work; they must be buried now. You will receive for the job the usual sum; in addition to that two quarts of brandy, and, for your back, a new pelisse. Is it a bargain?"

"A bargain," she answered. "I'll begin when you say;" and with arms akimbo and robust fists upon her hips, she regarded the defile of peasants and sledges rapidly discharging their score of dead. Her beautiful face remained impassive; pity seemed a stranger to those hard features, and yet what charm, what passion in those great black eyes, in that sensitive nose, in that firm, severe mouth!

The mayor counted the money into her hand, put the bottle of brandy on the snow beside her, and the sledges slowly drew on again, the peasants following in their wake as silently as they had come.

"But the pelisse?" demanded Milena.

"Tomorrow, when the work is done."

And the mayor also quitted the cemetery, and Milena took up her spade, and with a great swallow of brandy commenced to dig the first trench, crooning as she worked the words of an ancient grave-diggers song.

The sad melody, monotonous and slow as befitted the song of the dead, was accompanied by the dull ringing of the iron upon the frozen ground and the distant howling of the hungry wolves.

Another swallow of brandy, another swing of her muscular arms, and so it went on till the trench was done, and Milena, waiting a moment to regain her breath, gazed on the corpses.

"'Twas doubtless you," said she to an old man, with long white curls, clad in a rich cloak, trimmed with zibeline, and in whose girdle sparkled a superb yataghan, "'twas doubtless you who led the band. Well this time too, you shall go before!"

And she took him in her arms like a little child, descended into the trench herself and gently laid him on the ground. With the others she was not so ceremonious, an arm, a leg, a shoulder—anything, in short, that helped to lift and toss them to their bed in the ditch, served her purpose.

"But God help me!" she cried, suddenly, as before her in the snow lay stretched a bleeding trunk. "God help me if it isn't the Lord of Kamiez, that vile Turk and the oppressor of the poor!"

And she struck the face of the head that lay beside the trunk a blow which sent it rolling like a ball to the depths below.

Another swallow of brandy, a new body in the hole, then the grave securely closed, Milena was ready to begin the second.

In the meantime, the moon, rising higher and higher in the heavens, wrapped in its wan light the silent graves, the crucifix, the roofs of the now sleeping village, and the vast and soundless plain.

And again, the second trench ready, the gravedigger's daughter approached another group of dead. The face of the first one was covered with blood which had run from a cut in the head. At the same instant she heard a sigh—a long, shuddering breath that came from this body. Milena drew back hastily; courageous as she was, she felt her hair rise upon her head; and soon she saw that rigid body begin to stir.

He still lived, then. There was no longer a doubt of it! She caught him in her arms in order to succour him, rubbing with snow the face begrimed with blood and powder, and chafing his frozen hands. In a moment his eyes unclosed.

"Save me, Milena," he moaned, stretching his arms piteously towards her.

"Valerian," his name upon Milena's lips was half a scream and half a cry of menacing anger.

She shook her head brusquely, thrust him from her and rose to her feet.

"Save you!" she said, with a calm more terrible than either rage or the joy of a glutted vengeance; "when it is God that had delivered you in to my hands! You have betrayed me—you now belong to me! Pray to your God, Valerian, perhaps *He* will be merciful, but from me expect no pardon!"

"You have forgotten then, Milena, forgotten how I loved you!"

"No, I have forgotten nothing; but you, what have you done with all those vows? You, who ruined me, who then in spite of everything, left me for another! I shall not spare you, be sure of that, Valerian, be sure of that!"

"You will not kill me?" groaned the unhappy one.

"Kill you? No!" she smiled with a glacial irony which made him shudder. "I shall only do my duty—I shall bury you as I received order!"

"Bury me!" cried Valerian, "Bury me living?"

"Why not?" responded Milena, with a burst of cruel laughter. "I must earn the sheepskin for my back, which the mayor promised me."

60

"Have pity Milena, for God's sake have pity!"

"Did you have pity on me," she answered sternly "you who have vowed me to sorrow and to shame! This for your beautiful love—behold it."

And she seized him by the shoulders and sought to thrust him in; but he with that frightful death before him had risen to his feet, and a furious struggle began between them; a hopeless struggle, too, for soon Valerian renounced all thought of wrestling himself from the embrace of this savage creature. From loss of blood his strength was gone from him—he was but a child in her cruel hands.

"Mercy Milena, I beseech you, mercy!"

She responded with a disdainful foot-thrust which sent him rolling into the gaping hole. A last time he struggled to his feet, his arms outstretched, and clasping her knees with supplicating gesture.

But his prayers only rendered her even more ferocious still. She caught up her spade and struck his hands—their grasp relaxed, she struck again, a second, a third blow—he fell!

And Milena?

Milena, with one hand clenched upon her spade, the other doubled upon her hip, stood there and heard him groaning; stood there and contemplated him with cold, fierce eyes and voluptuous pleasure.

"Now," said she, "now, Valerian, are you mine."

Then she began to crumble the earth between her fingers and to fill the ditch, to fill it and stamp it down, as she had filled and stamped the first, her voice firm and as clear as ever, rising always to the chorus of her sinister song, and always accompanied by the sound of the clods falling one upon the other, by the ring of the spade, by the cawing crows circling hungrily above the heap of the unburied dead.

And in the East, the first grey lights of the coming morning slowly spread themselves across the heavens, pale and cold as the smile upon the faces of the frozen dead.

AN UNKNOWN WOMAN

THEY were speaking of their love adventures, and everyone was relating some strange ones—surprising and delightful meetings in a railway carriage, at a hotel, in foreign countries, at the sea-side.

According to Roger des Annettes, the latter was very favourable to love, but they asked the opinion of Gontran, who had not spoken, hitherto.

"After all, Paris is best," he said. "Women are just like chimney ornaments; we appreciate them the more when we find them in unlikely places, but one never meets with rare specimens except in Paris."

He remained silent for a few moments, and then continued:

"By Jove! It is very nice, after all. Just go into our streets, any fine morning. They seem to blossom just like flowers, those little women who trot along the pavement. Oh! what a pretty sight it is! One smells the violets as one walks along; the violets in the hand-barrows which the sellers push in front of them.

"The whole town is animated, and one looks at the women. How alluring they look in their thin dresses, which almost show their skin. One lounges on, with one's nose in the air, and in high spirits; one lounges, one looks out and watches. Ah! These mornings are very pleasant, and you see her coming in the distance and recognize her a hundred yards off, that particular woman who is going to captivate you. You guess it by the movement of her head and by her walk, and when she comes near to you, you say to yourself 'Look out, here is one' and you go towards her, devouring her with your eyes.

"Is she a shop-girl going on errands, or a young woman coming from church or going to her lover's rooms! That is of no consequence! Her breast shows its round, full outlines under her thin bodice. Oh! If one might only put one's hand on it; the hand or the lips. What does it matter whether her looks be bold or timid, whether she be dark or fair? The slightest touch of that woman sends a shiver down your back, and you long for her whom you have met thus, until evening! I have actually preserved the recollection of over twenty women whom I have seen once or ten times, in this fashion, and with whom I should have been madly in love, if I had known them more intimately.

"But there, a man never gets to know the woman he would dearly cherish. Have you ever noticed that? It is very strange! From time to time one sees a woman, the very sight of whom plays havoc with your desires, but one merely sees them, that is all. When I think of all the adorable creatures whom I have elbowed in the streets of Paris I feel inclined to go and hang myself. Where are they? Who are they? Where can I find them again, or see them again? A French proverb says that we often pass close to the side of happiness, and I am quite sure that I have often been close to the side of the woman who would have caught me like a linnet with the lure of her fresh, white skin."

Roger des Annettes had listened, smiling, and now he said:

"I know all about it, just as well as you do, and I will tell you what happened to me once. About five years ago I met for the first time, on the Pont de la Concorde, a tall, rather stout young woman who, created . . . well . . . who created a most astonishing effect on me. She was dark, dark and I might say, fat, with bright hair coming on her forehead, and with eyebrows which formed an arch from one temple to the other. A slight moustache on her lips made one dream . . . dream . . . like one dreams of woods which one loves, when one sees a nosegay, on the table. She had a very slender waist, whilst her full bust seemed to stand out as a challenge, and offered itself as a temptation to my sight. Her eyes were like spots of ink on white enamel. They were not eyes, but deep holes that were opened in her head, in the woman herself, through which one saw into her, penetrated into her. Oh! what a strange, opaque and empty look it was, without any ideas and yet so beautiful!

"I fancied that she was a Jewess. I followed her, and many men turned round to look at her, for she walked with a graceful, swinging gait, which rather excited the imagination. She took a cab in the Place de la Concorde, and I remained standing like a fool by the side of the Obelisque, seized by the most violent feelings of desire which had ever assailed me. I thought of her for at least three weeks, and then I forgot her.

"Six months later I met her again, in the Rue de la Paix, and when I saw her I experienced the same mental agitation as one does when one again meets a mistress whom one used to love so dearly, in days gone by. I stopped so as to have a good look at her as she came along, and when she passed so close as to touch me, I felt as if I were at the mouth of a furnace; and when she had gone a little distance, it seemed as if a cool wind were blowing on my face. I did not follow her, for I was afraid of committing some folly; I was afraid of myself.

"She often haunted my dreams; you know the kind of madness. I did not see her for a year, however, but then one evening, at sunset, I saw her walking in front of me in the Champs-Elysées, and I followed her with a mad wish to speak to her, to kneel before her, to tell her the emotions which were choking me, and I passed her twice, only to come back again, and twice, as I met her, I experienced that feeling of burning heat which had struck me in the Rue de la Paix.

"She looked at me, and then I saw her go into a house in the Rue de Presbury, and I waited for her for two hours under a gateway, but she did not come out, and so I made up my mind to question the porter; he did not, however, seem to understand me, and said that she must be merely a visitor.

"I did not see her again for eight months, and then, one bitterly cold morning, in January, I was walking along the Boulevard Malesherbes, almost running, in fact, to get warm, when I knocked up against her at a street corner, and made her drop a parcel. I was about to beg her pardon, when I saw it was she!

"At first I was silly with surprise, but then, having given her back what she had dropped, I said abruptly:

"'I am both sorry and delighted Madame, to have jostled you like this. I have known you and admired you now for two years, and have had the greatest longing to be introduced to you; but I could not find out who you are, or where you live. Excuse me for speaking thus, and pray attribute my words to the desire of being among the number of those who have the right of bowing to you, and I do not think that you can be offended with me for such feelings. You do not know me. I am Baron des Annett, and if you make enquiries about me, you will find out that I can be received in any society, and if you refuse my request, you will make me most unhappy. Come, be kind, and tell me how and where I can see you.'

"'She looked at me fixedly with her strange, cold eyes, and then said with a smile:

"'Give me your address. I will come and see you.'

"I was so surprised that I must have shown it, but I soon recover from such shocks, and so I immediately gave her my card, which, she put into her pocket with a rapid movement of the hand, which was evidently accustomed to hiding letters, and so I grew bold and said:

"'When shall I see you again?'

She hesitated, as if she were making a complicated calculation and no doubt she was trying to recollect how she was going to employ her time from hour to hour, and then she whispered: "'Sunday morning, if that will suit you?'

"'I should rather think it would!'

"And then she left me, after having scanned me, judged me, weighed me and analysed me, with that searching and undefined look which seems to leave something on the skin, a kind of sticky substance, as if it had ejected one of those inky liquids which the scuttle fish uses in order to cloud the water, and to send its prey to sleep.

"Until the Sunday I devoted my thoughts to trying to find out who she was and to making up my mind how I should act with regard to her. Should I pay her, and how? And finally, I determined to buy her a beautiful piece of jewellery, which I put on the mantel-piece, in its case, and then I waited for her, after having passed an almost sleepless night.

"'At about ten o'clock she came, perfectly calm and tranquil, and gave me her hand just as if she had known me for a long time. I made her sit down, and helped her of with her bonnet, her veil, her fur, and her muff, and then I began to show myself rather more gallant, though I did so with a certain amount of embarrassment, for I had no time to lose.

"However, she did not require much pressing; we had scarcely exchanged a dozen words before I began to undress her, but she herself finished that difficult job, which I can never manage successfully. I always prick my fingers, I knot all the strings instead of untying them, I bungle at everything, I lose time and my head as well.

"Oh! my dear friend, do you know any more delicious moments in your whole life than those when one looks, at a distance and from motives of discretion, so as not to alarm that ostrich-like modesty which they all possess—at the woman who is taking off all her rustling clothes one after the other, and letting them fall at her feet for your sake?

"And what is prettier than to see their motions in disembarrassing themselves of those soft garments which fall gently to the ground, as if they had been struck by death? How beautiful and attractive is the sight of her skin, of her bare arms, and of her bosom after she has taken off her stays, and how exciting are the outlines of her body, which can be discerned beneath the last veil!

But suddenly I saw something surprising, a large black spot between her shoulders, for she had turned her back to me; it was a large, very black spot in relief. I had, however, promised her not to look at her.

"What was it? Of course I could not doubt my eyes, and the recollection of her visible moustache, of her eyebrows that met and of her mass of hair which was like a helmet on her head, ought to have prepared me for this surprise. However, I was stupefied, and suddenly seized by strange visions and reminiscences. I thought that I had before me one of those witches in *The Arabian Nights*, one of those dangerous and perfidious creatures whose mission it is to drag men down into unknown abysses. I thought of Solomon, who made the Queen of Sheba walk over glass, to make sure that her legs were straight.

"And . . . when it came to singing my love song, I discovered I had no voice, not a single note, my friend. Yes, I beg your pardon, I had the voice of a Papal chorister, at which she was at first surprised, and then absolutely angry, for she said, as she was dressing herself again:

"'It was quite useless to trouble one for this!'

"I tried to make her accept the ring I had bought for her, but she said 'What do you take me for, Monsieur?' so haughtily, that I got red to my ears under this accumulation of humiliations. And she left the room without another word.

"That is the whole of my adventure, but the worst of it is that now I am in love with her, madly in love. I never see a woman without thinking of her. All others are repugnant to me and disgust me, unless they are like her, and I cannot kiss a woman's cheek without seeing hers by the side of it, and without suffering horribly from the unappeased desire which tortures me.

"She is present at all my meetings with my mistresses, and spoils their caresses and makes them odious to me. She is always there, dressed or naked, as if she were my real mistress; she is there, close to the other one, standing up or in bed, visible but unseizable. And now I believe that she was a woman bewitched, who had a mysterious talisman between her shoulders.

"I do not even now know who she is. I have met her twice since and bowed to her, but she did not return my salute, and pretended not to know me. Who is she? An Asiatic, very likely? No doubt an Eastern Jewess? Yes, a Jewess! I have an idea that she is a Jewess. But why? Well there! I do not know!"

THE MYSTERIOUS LITTLE MILLINER

ON one of those beautiful, cold, bright days in winter, when the ugliest eaves of a house and the most beautiful friezes are alike covered with sparkling diamonds of ice, and all the places near Vienna where skating was to be had were covered with elegantly dressed male and female skaters, Felix W——, who was a poor, but young and good-looking student, had lost his way in the Schwarzenberg gardens, and was still there when the gate was closed to promenaders, and the cream of the Viennese aristocracy gave themselves up to the amusement of skating on the glittering surface of the well-known small pond. The student remained standing at a modest distance from the aristocratic clique, and enjoyed, which was to him, the unusual sight of the beautiful women and girls, who glided hither and thither in velvet dresses, trimmed with costly fur, showing their pretty little feet as they skated, or else were sitting comfortably in hand-sledges, and were being pushed about by gentlemen. When he left the garden, the gigantic porter in a thick, shaggy fur coat, which made him look like

a Polar bear, who was keeping guard over that aristocratic sanctuary, looked at his shabby clothes in open-
eyed astonishment, and at last asked him, roughly:

"How did you get in"

"Just like everybody else did," the student replied
with a smile; "through the gate."

The porter muttered an oath.

"It is strictly prohibited to let anybody in at this
time of day," he said, "and I shall be found fault with
on your account, that is quite certain."

The student put his hand near the breast-pocket
of his shabby greatcoat, with the magnanimous inten-
tion, to appease the man's wrathful soul with a small
tip, but he declined the gift with a majestic wave of
his hand.

"I will not accept anything from you," he growled;
"but don't let it happen again."

Felix W—— then went away, and had soon forgotten all about the occurrence in the Schwarzenberg
garden; who then can describe his astonishment,
when a few days later he read the following notice in
the first column of a Viennese news-paper:

"The gentleman who witnessed the aristocratic company skating in the Schwarzenberg garden,
on the **th of this month, is requested to be in the
Ringstrasse, between the Schwarzenberg square, and
the prolongation of the Kärtnerstrasse, at five o'clock
tomorrow evening, as somebody has an important
communication to make to him."

Felix could not for a moment doubt, that that notice was intended for him, so the next day he dressed
himself more carefully than usual, and even sacrificed

a shilling on the altar of a hairdresser, to be shaved and have his hair cut. Smelling of pomatum and scent from head to foot, he waited for the unknown fair one at the appointed time, for as a child of the great city on the Danube, he felt sure that the "important communication" would be made to him by a woman, and by a pretty woman.

The clock of St. Stephen's Cathedral was striking five, and the other clocks were following suit in various tones, when a small, pretty female figure came up to the student, and gave him a little gloved hand and in a clear melodious, roguish voice said "Thank you."

"What for?"

"For coming."

"Could I possibly have done anything else than obey such a charming summons?"

"But you could not know . . ."

"Oh! I guessed immediately . . . that it was a lady and a beautiful lady, who summoned me here."

By this time they were walking side by side towards the Openring.

"But suppose your presentiment has deceived you, and I am old and ugly"

"That is impossible."

The unknown lady laughed, and at the same time two large dark eyes, flashed at the handsome student through the thick, black veil, which covered her face.

"No, no you are young and pretty!" he cried.

"Well, yes," she replied, "I am young and pretty, people even say very pretty—but let us say pretty. Yes, we will say pretty," she continued, "but for Heaven's sake don't imagine that I am a lady; I am only a Milliner's girl."

"So much the better," the student exclaimed; "then we are more on an equality, and I need not be afraid lest you should disappear just as suddenly as you have come to me unexpectedly."

"Well, now tell me something about yourself, your life and your circumstances,' the girl said.

"Very gladly, but how can that interest you?"

"Everything that relates to you, interests me," the unknown female replied.

The student then told her that he was the son of small tradespeople, and had been brought up to the same business; that after his father's death he left his master and began to study, whilst he only just managed to keep himself by copying and giving lessons, he told her that by these means he had managed to get to the University, and also, that now that he was a barrister, he still had a very hard struggle to live.

"And have you already been in love often?" the veiled lady asked.

"Never as yet."

"You are not telling me the truth."

"Why should I deceive you?" he said.

"Our peculiar code of morals allows that to a man in the fullest measure, which it looks upon as a sin in a woman."

"So you have really never yet been in love?" she said in a rapid, enigmatical, urgent voice.

"Never yet."

She began to laugh again.

"What are you laughing about?"

"I was only thinking . . ." she hesitated and laughed again. "I will tell you another time," she added "now I will tell you about myself."

She related a biography to him, which resembled his own to a hair. Poverty, work, a struggle for her daily bread; and she painted her means as small and insufficient, that the student gave a doubting look at her black silk dress, and at her somewhat worn, but valuable shawl.

"My appearance does not seem to you to agree with my words," she said quickly, as she noted his suspicions, "but I think a good deal of myself, and would rather deny myself everything else, as long as I am always nicely dressed"

"Will you now permit me to see your face, which I am sure must be charming?" Felix asked.

"Not today."

"Suppose I ask you very prettily."

"What do you call asking prettily?"

"On my knees."

"What are you thinking of, here in the street!"

"Why not?"

"No, no, I will take the kneeling as done," the unknown replied roguishly, "and I will raise my veil underneath the next lamp post, but only for a moment, so remember and have a good look."

She really did as she had promised, and threw back her veil with a knowing smile. It certainly was only for a moment, but in that moment the unfortunate student's peace of mind was utterly destroyed; he had never before seen such a beautiful charming female face, such highly bred features, joined to such flesh, alluring beauty and piquant, mischievous looks.

"Did you look at me carefully?" she said.

"Oh! yes."

"Well, what do you think of me?"

"You have bewitched me by a single look; I am in love."

"So suddenly!" she asked, in a mocking voice.

"Madly in love," he continued, whilst she laughed, and said in a whisper:

"If I take half of it as true, may I tell you that I like you also very much, and that the next time we meet I will allow you to accompany me home, where . . . but I have said too much already, so goodbye for today."

"When shall I see you again?"

"I will let you know through the same paper. Adieu!"

She walked away quickly, with short, elastic steps, crossed the street and went towards the inner town. He looked after her until she was out of sight, and then he returned to his modest little room, with his heart full of sweet hopes, and read law by the glaring light of his petroleum lamp.

A tedious week passed, during which Felix read that unlucky paper through twice every day, which always contained so many assignations, but none for him, until one morning his heart beat in joyful impatience, when he saw the notice:

To the gentleman of the Schwarzenberg garden. Tomorrow at five o'clock, at the same place.

Felix was again punctual, and this time he had got on a new silk tie and kid gloves, and again, as the clock struck five, the unknown beauty appeared.

"Let us take a cab," she said, so they took the first fiacre they met, and the little milliner told him to drive to a street in a distant suburb. During the drive, the student and the pretty girl had already become

76

more intimate, for just before the cab stopped at the house which she had mentioned, Felix had boldly thrown his arms round her, and their lips met in their first, blissful kiss. She got out first and paid the driver, evidently very liberally, for he took off his hat down to the ground and said:

"I kiss your hand, *Fräulein*."

"Follow me," she whispered to Felix, and then ran upstairs to the third floor, where she opened a door and the student struck a match, whilst she locked it again behind him.

"Now we will be happy," she cried in ecstasy, took off her bonnet and shawl, so that her thick, golden curls fell down over her back like golden snakes, and threw her arms ardently round the poor student's neck, who felt a flood of bliss, such as he had never experienced before, pervade him. Whilst she laid the tea table, he sat sideways on a chair, and feasted his eyes on her graceful, alluring movements, and listened to the strange, exciting rustle of her silk dress, which fitted closely to her slim, but splendidly developed form, they really were happy! They chattered like two innocent, merry children, and enjoyed their meal, and teased and kissed each other. Then they grew silent, he lay at her feet, and he pressed his burning face to her heaving bosom.

The lamp grew dimmer and dimmer, until it went quite out.

They met nearly every third day, and at last the little milliner expressed a wish to go to a ball at Sperl's.

"I have never been to a place of that kind," she said with a peculiar smile; "and I should very much like for once to see what goes on there."

Felix immediately declared that he was quite ready to accompany her, and the next Sunday they accordingly went. The student's mistress, in rather short petticoats and charmingly shod, a thorough Viennese milliner, created a great sensation; her dark eyes glistened with unwonted fire, beneath her powdered hair, and she danced like a Bacchante or a Mænad, and as she was whirling past in the arms of a handsome cadet of hussars, two fashionably dressed gentlemen came up to the student.

"Excuse me," one of them said with a polite bow, "but who is the lady whom you are with?"

"The student gave them the first name he could think of, and the gentleman who had asked turned to the other and said:

"It is very strange, but what a striking likeness! In any other place, I should have sworn that it was Countess X——."

Months passed in undisturbed and unmeasured poetical happiness. The student loved the little milliner more every day, and indulged in the boldest plans. As soon as he had obtained an appointment he would marry her, and already he used to picture their married life to himself as a perfect idyll.

The girl let him do as he liked, with an enigmatical smile that was half mocking, half sad, until one day she remained away for good. In vain did Felix beseech her through notices in every paper; in vain did he perambulate the streets continually. He could learn nothing of her, and when he asked after her at her lodgings, he was told that she had moved, but nobody knew where.

Two years had passed, when one day Felix happened to be going by the new Opera house at the moment when the performance was over. He wanted to cross the road, but a carriage was in his way, and at that moment his Unknown, wrapped in ermine from head to foot and radiant with beauty, came out of the Opera house leaning on the arm of an elderly man.

She saw him also, but she merely gave him a careless glance, as if she had never seen him, and never rested on his breast. He knew enough. He had wasted his best and highest feelings on a woman from the Olympus of the upper classes, who was surfeited with pleasure. He had been the plaything of an aristocratic Messalina; nothing more!

ÇA IRA

I WENT to Barvieller simply because had I read in a guide-book: "*Feris Museum, two Rubens, a Teniers, a Ribena*." And I thought I would go and see them; I could dine at the Hôtel de l'Europe, which the guide-book said was excellent, and leave again the next day.

"The museum was closed, it is not opened except at the request of travellers, but it was for me, and I was enabled to look at a few daubs, which an imaginative keeper had attributed to the greatest masters of painting, but when I had done that, I found myself quite alone, in the long street of a small, strange town, built in the middle of an endless plain, and having absolutely nothing to do, I walked up and down this *artery* and looked at the few, poor shops, and then, as it was only four o'clock, I was seized with one of those fits of dejection which send the most energetic people silly. What was I to do? I would have given five hundred francs for any kind of distraction! As, however, I could think of nothing whatever, I made up my mind to smoke a good cigar, and I went to look for a tobacconist's, which I soon found. The woman who kept the shop gave me several boxes to choose from, and having looked at the cigars, which I guessed were detestable, I accidentally looked at the shopkeeper.

She was a stout woman of about forty-five, and was growing grey, and had a fat, respectable face, which seemed familiar to me, but yet I did not know her. No, certainly not. But perhaps I might have met her somewhere formerly? That was possible. She must be some old acquaintance whom I had lost sight of for some time, and who had no doubt changed and got enormously stout.

"I beg your pardon, Madame, for looking at you so hard, but I fancy I knew you years ago."

She blushed a little and said:

"It is very strange . . . but I thought the same."

"All right!" I shouted, but she raised her hands in horror at the voice, and said:

"If anybody were to hear you . . ." And then she said in her turn: "Why it is you, George!" And then she looked round in some alarm, lest she might be heard, but we were quite alone.

How could I have recognized poor, thin, unhappy, Ça ira in this stout and tranquil tobacconist?

How many recollections that name suddenly awakened in me: Bourgival, La Grenouillère, Chatou Fourmaise's restaurant, long days in a boat, ten years of my life spent in this part of the country, on this delightful part of the river.

There were a dozen of us at that time living at Chatou in a strange fashion, always half-naked and half-drunk. Boatmen's morals have very much changed nowadays. They wear eye glasses.

Our band possessed a score of boat-women, regular and irregular. On certain Sundays we had the society of four of them, on others we had them all. Some lived there, so to say, and the others came when they had nothing better to do. Five or six lived at the expense of the others on the men without wives, and Ça ira was one of them.

She was a poor, thin girl, with a limp, which made her look like a grasshopper. She was very timid, and awkward in everything she did. She fastened timidly on to the humblest, the least thought of and the poorest of us, who kept her for a day or a month according to his means. How she came amongst us, nobody remembered. Had one of us met her, some evening when he was drunk, at the Boatman's Ball and taken her off, as we did sometimes? Had we invited her to lunch, when we saw her sitting by herself, at a small table in the corner? None of us could tell, but she formed part of our band.

We had christened her Ça ira because she was always complaining of fate, of her bad luck, of her disappointments. Every Sunday we used to say to her: "Well, Ça ira, are things going on all right?" And she invariably replied: "No, not very well, but I must hope that it will all come right someday."

It was a mystery how that poor, awkward, unpleasant-looking creature could ever have come to exercise the calling that really requires the most grace, skill, cunning and beauty, but Paris is full of frail women who are ugly enough to frighten a gendarme.

What did she do during the other six days of the week! She had several times told us that she worked, but at what we did not know, and were quite indifferent about her means of subsistence.

"Then, I had almost entirely lost sight of her. Our group had gradually become broken up, making way for another generation to whom we had also left Ça ira. I heard of her when I went to lunch at Fourmaise's, from time to time. Our successors, who did not know why we had given her that name, had thought it was an Oriental name, and christened her Zaira; then in their turn they had given up their boats and a few boat women to the succeeding generation. (A generation of boating men generally lives for three years on the water, and then leaves the Seine to become a magistrate, a medical man or a politician).

Then Zaira had become Zara, and later, Zara became modified into Sarah. Then she was taken for a Jewess, and the last of all, those who wore eye-glasses, simply called her the Jewess.

Then she disappeared, and now I had found her again in the tobacco shop at Barviller.

"How are things going now?' I asked her.

"Rather better," she replied and I felt great curiosity to learn all about her life. Formerly, I should not have dreamt of it, but now I was puzzled, attracted and altogether interested, and I said:

"How did you manage to have any luck?"

"I do not know. It came to me when I least expected it."

"Did it befall you at Chatou?"

"Oh! No!"

"Where then?"

"In Paris, in a large house where I was living."

"Ah! So you had a place in Paris?"

"Yes, I was at Madame Ravel the fashionable dressmaker in the Rue de Rivoli."

And she began to give me a thousand details about her past life, secrets of Parisian life, about the interior of a dressmaker's establishment, how the shop-girls lived, their thoughts, the whole history of a work girl's heart, that hawk which hunts in the streets in the morning when going to work, at midday, when sauntering about bareheaded after dinner, and at night, when one is going home, and she said, pleased at having an opportunity of speaking about former days:

"If you only knew how nasty they are and what they do. We used to tell each other what we had been up to, every day. We made fun of the men, you know.

"The first trick that I was guilty of was about an umbrella. I had an old alpaca one, an umbrella to be ashamed of. One day, as I was closing it on my arrival, tall Louise said to me:

"'What! Do you venture out with a thing like that!'

"'I have no other, and just now my funds are low. My funds always were low.'

"She replied, however, 'Go and get one at the Madeleine. We all of us get them from there; one can get as many as one wants. It is perfectly simple.'

"And she explained it to me; so after lunch I went to the Madeleine with Irma, and we went to the sacristan and told him that we had left at umbrella behind us the week before. He asked us what the handle was like, and we said it had an agate knob, and then he took us into a room where there were over fifty lost umbrellas; we looked at them all, but could not find mine, but I singled out a very handsome one, with a carved ivory handle, and Louise went and claimed it a few days later. She described it before seeing it, and they gave it to her without any hesitation. To do that, however, one had to be dressed very well."

She laughed a little, and then went on: "Oh! we were up to some very funny tricks. There were five of us in the work-room, four of us ordinary, and Irma, who was beautiful. She looked highly-bred, and had a lover who was a state councillor, but that did not make her stick to him. One winter she said to us, you know, 'we will have a good bit of fun.' And she told us her idea.

"You know, Irma's carriage and gait would turn the head of any man, and then her figure and her hips would make their mouth water, so she formed a plan for each of us to make a hundred francs to buy a ring apiece, and this is how she did it.

"I was not rich at the time, as you may know, any more than the rest, for we only got a hundred francs a month in the shop, and that did not go far. Of course, we each of us had two or three lovers, who gave us a little, but not much. When we went out in the middle of the day, we sometimes hooked a gentleman who came again the next day; one kept him dangling about for a fortnight, and then one yielded, but they never brought in much, and we only took those from Chatou for pleasure. Oh! If you knew the tricks we were up; it was enough to make anyone die of laughter. So when Irma proposed to put us in the way of making a hundred francs, we all got excited.

What I am that going to tell you is very bad, but that does not matter; you know life, and then, when one has lived at Chatou for four years . . .

"'Well,' she said to us, 'we will pick up the best men in Paris at the Opera ball, the most distinguished and violent, I know them.'

"We did not think it was true at first because those sort of men are not made for milliner's girls: for Irma yes, but not for us. Oh! she was a swell, was Irma. You know, in the work-room we used to say that if the Emperor had known her, he would certainly have married her.

"She made us put on our very best things, and said to us: 'You must not go to the ball, but you must each of you remain in a separate cab in the neighbouring streets. A gentleman will come and get into your cab, and as soon as he is in you must kiss him as nicely as you can, and then you must scream out loud, to show that you have made a mistake, and were expecting somebody else. It will inflame the pigeons, to see that he has got somebody else's place, and he will try and remain by force: you must resist and try to get rid of him . . . and then you will go and have supper with him . . . And he will be bound to pay you handsomely."

"Don't you understand yet? Well, this is what she did. She made us all four get into four different, well-appointed cabs, and then she stationed us in the streets near the Opera, and went to the ball by herself. As she knew the names of the chief men of note in Paris, because our employer made their wives dresses, she chose one first of all, in order to puzzle him. She said all sorts of things to him, for she is very witty, and when she saw that he was properly hooked, she took off her mask, and he was caught in the net. Of course, he wanted to take her off immediately, but she made an appointment with him in half-an-hour in a cab opposite No. 20 Rue Taitbout. I was in that cab; I was well wrapped up, and had a veil on, and so when a gentleman suddenly put his head in at the window and said: 'Is that you?' I replied in a low voice: 'Yes, it is I; get in quickly'; and as soon as he was in I kissed him, I kissed him so as to take away his breath, and then I continued: 'Oh! how happy I am! How happy I am!' And then suddenly I exclaimed: 'But it is not you! Oh! good heavens! good heavens!' And I began to cry.

"You may guess how embarrassed the man was! He tried to console me, however, and protested that he had also made a mistake!

"I went on crying, but not so violently, and I uttered deep sighs, and then he said very pretty things to me. He was a perfect gentleman, and he was glad to see I was crying less violently, until from one thing to the other, he asked me to go and have supper with him. I refused, and wanted to jump out of the carriage, but he put his arm round my waist and pulled me back, and then he kissed me, just as I had kissed him, when he got in, and then we went . . . we went . . . and had super, you understand . . . and he gave me . . . he gave me five hundred francs! . . . Some men are generous.

"Well, the affair turned out well for all of us; Louise had the least, and she had two hundred francs. But you know Louise is really too thin!"

The tobacconist went on, pouring out all her recollections which had been shut up for so long in her
breast. All the past, its poverty and its amusing sides
stirred her heart. She regretted the fast and Bohemian
life of the pavement in Paris made up of privations
and of bought caresses, of laughter and of wretched-
ness, of cunning tricks, and of real love, at times, and
I asked her how she had obtained her tobacco shop.
She smiled and said:

"Oh! that is quite a long story. You must know that
in the house where I lived, in the next room to me, a
law-student lived, one of those students who do nothing. He lived in a café from morning till night, and
was more passionately fond of billiards than anybody
I have ever met, and when I was alone, we sometimes
spent the evening together. I had Roger by him."

"Who is Roger?"

"My son."

"Ah!"

"He made me a small allowance on which to bring
up the boy, but I felt quite certain that he would never
be any real good to me, for I never saw such a lazy
man. At the end of ten years he had not yet passed
his first examination, and when his family saw that
nothing could be done with him, they called him into
the country, but we have kept up a correspondence
because of the child. And then, just imagine, at the
last election two years ago, I heard that he had been
elected Deputy, and he has spoken in the Chamber.
Certainly, as they say, amongst the blind, the one-eyed
is king. But to cut my story short, I went to see him,
and he got me this tobacco shop, as the daughter of a

convict. It is true that my father was transported, but I never thought that that would be of any service to me. However . . . But here is Roger."

A tall, correctly dressed, grave young man came into the room, and kissed his mother's forehead, and she said to me:

"This is my son, Monsieur. He is head of the Mansion-house. He will be a sub-prefect in time."

I bowed to that functionary, and I took my leave and returned to my hotel, after having gravely shaken hands with *Ça ira*.

A CRUEL TEST

THE altered position of woman is greatly respon-
sible for our social evils, which are growing worse
and becoming more threatening every day. As long
as she fulfils her destined part as wife, mother, and
mistress of the house, she is man's companion in joy
and sorrow, in poverty and wealth, but as soon as she
quits that sphere, she can only become the slave or
the ruler of the man. Therefore, the evils of modern
society which threaten all our institutions, are least
apparent amongst those who bear the honourable
title of the working classes.

People of rank, wealthy women, who never need
to give a thought to their daily bread, and who never work, are in consequence of their idleness and
semi-education, most prone to strive for that freedom
which soon degenerates into licentiousness, to hand
over their family duties to others, and in exchange,
try strange and frivolous experiments with their own
happiness, and that of others.

The heroine of our story was a lady of this sort,
for whom the French have invented the delightful
expression, *femme imcomprise*—a woman who is not

understood. Adele von Geierburg, had never enjoyed the blessing of a mother's education. She had been launched into the world after passing through the hands of a wet nurse, a nurse, a governess, and a dancing and music master—a thorough Viennese—a pampered, spoilt girl, full of pretensions, but without anything to back them up, had been married to an old man, and after his death, when she was only five and twenty, she found herself left a rich, healthful widow, with many admirers, free, but tired of pleasures, and having lost all her ideals, and all her better feelings. Life appeared to her to be a mere burden; and her only business, that of getting rid of her time in one way or another, seemed to her a labour of the Danaides. And yet, in spite of all her mental lassitude, and of the void in her heart, she raised the sweetest illusions in every man who came near her, and excited the most passionate longing to possess her in all men who were brought in contact with her.

It is a delusion to which men are very liable, to think that every woman who is beautiful, and whose eyes are brighter than others, must also be witty and impressionable; that he expects to find the poetry which envelops her person in her mind as well, and Adele was very beautiful, and her whole appearance bore a strong impression of everything in which her soul was so deficient. She was of middle height and slender, though her figure was not deficient in round, and even voluptuous softness, and the blue veins were distinctly visible through her dazzlingly white and delicate skin. Her features were beautiful, with a classic nose, and a small, rosy mouth, and an abundant mass of bright, light hair formed the golden frame of her lovely face. But her eyes were the most wonderful thing about her, those large blue eyes, which had a dreamy look in them on fine days, and which, from time to time, were almost supernaturally bright.

She had spent her year of mourning in travelling and had visited Italy, the South of France and Spain, and was now at that lovely place Meran, where she was enjoying the deep green of the German forests, and the beauty of the Tyrolese hills. She had soon brought together all the aristocratic elements of that watering-place in her drawing-room, where they danced and sang, had good—or bad—music, and undertook excursions together on horse or donkey-back to all the beautiful places in the neighbourhood. Adele, however, preferred to have a horse or donkey which she had tried, and therefore knew, saddled, and so roam about the mountains, without even a guide.

Once the fancy took her to go to St. Catherine's, that little church which looks down on Meran from the high rock, amidst the deep snow, whilst the laurel trees are green below. She reached the village safely, gave her pony to the landlord, put on her fur jacket, which she had taken the precaution to bring with her, and then, armed with an Alpine stick, she began to scramble about amongst the picturesque rocks. By degrees she got farther and farther from her starting place, and mounted higher and higher, until the setting sun admonished her that it was time to return. Then, however, she discovered that she had missed the path, and lost her way in the wild ravines, in which the snow was still lying deep. She tried in vain to find the road out until at last she got to a steep wall of rock and could neither go backwards nor forwards, neither ascend nor descend. She called out loud, and discharged a pocket pistol which she had in the pocket of her fur jacket, but the repeated echo was her only answer: no human voice was to be heard, and at last she lost courage, sat down on a great piece of rock, from which she had first of all to brush off the snow, and began to cry.

One quarter of an hour passed after the other; the sun had already set behind the hills and a cold wind was whistling amongst the bare rocks and roughly blowing about Adele's golden curls; and she did what she had not thought of doing for years, she began to pray.

Suddenly she heard a human voice close to her: "For Heaven's sake what are you doing here? However did you get up to this spot?"

Adele sprang up; a young man was standing on the rock above her, and now politely took his hat off to her, and in a few words she told him about her adventure and situation.

"May I offer you my help?" the stranger said with a smile.

"How can you ask? I beg you to assist me. You have come to me, like the angel did to the Emperor Maximillian on the Martius-Wand," Adele replied.

With a bold leap the stranger was at her side, and to gather from his dress and weapons, he appeared to be a sportsman, but she who was usually so proud, did not think anything about that matter, but panting and leaning on his arm she began the descent. For some time everything went well and already Adele saw the church tower of St. Catherine at no great distance,

when her foot slipped and she wrenched her ankle not
badly, but just so, that at the moment she could not
use her foot.

"Allow me to carry you," the stranger said, who
quickly collected himself.

"I do not know . . ." Adele stammered.

"Do you really intend to be prudish here, and situated as you are," the hunter asked with a smile.

"No, no,' she exclaimed, "but I am afraid of being
too much trouble to you."

"Pray do not mention that!" the stranger said, and
without saying anything more, he took his lovely burden into his arms.

Adele felt a strange sensation, as she lay against the
breast of the man who had immediately made such an
impression upon her as no other man had ever done,
and felt his heart beating quickly against hers, and his
breath on her cheeks. Was it love that she felt?

And what of him, the stranger? A new world had
opened itself to him in the wonderful eyes of that
lovely, fair-haired woman, and love's arrow was in his
heart, and as he held her in his arms, he continually
drove it deeper and deeper in. When he had seen
Adele back to the inn where she had left her horse, she
took his hand and thanked him in the most exaggerated terms. Meanwhile, it had grown dark, and so the
stranger offered to accompany her down to Meran.
Adele looked at him with doubt and hesitation.

"So that you may know on whom you are be-
stowing your confidence," he said, when he noticed
her embarrassment, "allow me to introduce myself
to you." He gave her his card, on which she read:
Friedrich von Warndorf.

"You are a Russian, if I am not mistaken," the baroness said. "I have heard your name mentioned in society."

Warndorf told her that that was the case. He belonged to a German family, who had estates in Courland, had been travelling for years, and was now amusing himself by running about the Tyrolean mountains with his gun over his shoulder, and thus it was that he had met Adele. He was still young, and tall and strongly built; his expressive, sunburnt face, which was set in a long, light beard bore the stamp of resolute manliness and of passions. After they had some refreshment the Russian assisted Adele into the saddle, and went before her to show her the way, whilst she rode behind him at a foot-pace.

From time to time they exchanged a few words, but both were too much taken up with themselves: and their own peculiar sensations to be able to enter into any lengthy conversation. It was very late when they arrived at the villa at Obermais, where Adele was staying. With another pressure of the hand, and a friendly invitation on her part to come and see her, they separated. The very next day Warndorf called on the baroness. She could not use her foot yet, so was consequently at home, and received her rescuer in the heartiest manner, as she lay on her couch, and begged him to keep her company. He agreed to do so, with the greatest pleasure, and he told her about his travels in South America and Africa, and read her a couple of stories by Iwan Turgenjew, the gifted Russian writer.

Adele was confined to the house for several days, and during all that time she would only allow

Warndorf to leave her for very short periods, as she enjoyed his conversation, and told him so openly and when she could go to the Promenade again, the Russian was her constant companion; she began to make mountain excursions in his company, and he was her guest at tea nearly every evening.

The world had been talking about them, their intimacy and their probable marriage, long before they had come to an understanding. One evening they were sitting on the terrace of the inn at Schloss Tirol; and were looking at the distant mountains which were glowing in the setting sun.

"We shall also have to separate soon," Adele began.

"Why?" Warndorf asked.

"I have been away from home long enough," Adele replied, "and important business calls me back, and you, I suppose, you also, will soon be returning . . ."

"If you send me away," he said in a low voice.

"What are you thinking of," Adele said hastily. "I shall find it very hard to do without your society."

"Baroness . . . you . . . you say that . . ." the Russian stammered.

"Is it not natural that I should . . . ?" and a long, languishing look from her lovely blue eyes accompanied her words.

"Do not be angry with me," Warndorf began, "if I avail myself of your favourable feelings towards me, to tell you what has been in my heart for a long time."

"Well?"

"I love you, Adele!"

The beautiful woman started.

"Do not reject me, until you have heard me to the end," he said.

"But you know that I no longer believe in love," she replied in a low voice.

"I know it," Warndorf said, "and on that very account I have never nourished the hope that you could return my feelings for you. But you have told me repeatedly that you are living an objectless life, without any enjoyment or any pleasure, so what I want to ask you is, live with me. Allow me to convince you of the sincerity and the depth of my feelings, put me to any test, and if I stand the ordeal, and if perhaps you feel a little liking for me give me your hand in marriage."

Adele looked down into the valley where the shadows were growing deeper, without giving him an answer; the Russian also was silent for some time, and then he took her hand.

"Adele," he said in a supplicating voice, "decide over my life and death; only one word."

"Over life and death?" she replied with a smile.

"Yes, over life and death," Warndorf repeated; "for if you cannot love me, I would rather die."

"That is a mere phrase . . ." the lovely heartless woman said, with a contemptuous curl of her lips.

"No, Adele, I am perfectly in earnest, so decide," the impassioned man replied. "It's for you to decide."

"Very well," she said; "I will give you a year, and if you succeed in convincing me that there is such a thing as real love, and in winning my heart, I will be yours. But if you fail in your undertaking then . . . you must kill yourself!" And she began to laugh heartily.

"Do not make a joke of the matter," Warndorf said "If in a year's time you tell me that I am condemned to live without you, then you will pronounce my death sentence, and I shall only have one wish more . . ." and he hesitated.

"What is it?" the baroness asked.

"To die by your hand," the Russian replied.

"Well, you shall have that pleasure," Adele said

"You would be capable . . . ?" he stammered.

"Of killing you? Why not? I should be just as capable of doing it, as you would be of committing suicide on my account."

"Then you still doubt . . . ?"

She shrugged her shoulders.

"Give me your word, that in a year you will either marry me, or kill me," the Russian continued.

"Very well, I will take you at your word," Adele said, with strange haste. "If I do not love you in a year, I shall have the right to sentence you to death and to carry out my sentence myself. Do not forget it."

"No," Warndorf replied.

"And do not reckon on finding any mercy with me," Adele continued.

"No, I will have you or die."

They gave each other their hands, and the gloomy compact was sealed. The year was over. The beautiful widow had spent it with her admirer, partly on her estate in Bohemia, partly at her mansion in Vienna and lastly on the Lago Maggiore. It was spring once more, and they were standing on the verandah of her villa on Isola Bella, and instead of the lovely valley of Meran, the deep blue lake glistened at their feet in the evening sun.

"It is getting cool, let us go in," she said, and going into the small drawing room, she lay down carelessly on a couch, while Warndorf closed the doors and made up the fire on the open hearth.

"You seem to have forgotten," she began.

"What?"

"Our compact. Today, is the day."

"Today . . . !"

A cold shiver ran down Warndorf's back.

"Come to me," Adele said in a whisper. "Close, quite close."

The Russian obeyed her, and his heart beat violently.

"I suppose you are curious to know what I have to say to you today."

"I am trembling . . ."

"Hard as I have tried to doubt the depth and sincerity of your feelings for me, you have succeeded in persuading me that there is such a thing as real love, and that you love me. You have conquered me . . ."

"Adele," the enraptured man exclaimed, and threw himself at her feet.

"You have conquered me," Adele repeated, laying her hand on his shoulder, whilst a tender fire, which gave promise of unspeakable raptures, "but not altogether . . ." she added, after a pause, with some hesitation.

"What do you mean?"

"I believe now, that you love me," the heartless coquette continued, with cutting coldness, "but I cannot share your feelings."

"Adele . . . you are cruel."

"I am only open and honest."

"Very well, then, let me die," Warndorf said, in a hollow and resigned voice.

"Do you think that I have forgotten our compact?"
Adele continued, with a demoniacal laugh. "Your life
is in my hands, and I am not the woman to make
you a present of it. I myself am incapable of love, but
it gives me pleasure to be loved so madly as you love
me, and to see the man who loves me, and whom I
despise, die at my feet."

"Are you in earnest?" the horrified Russian asked.

"You do not believe it?" she replied in a mocking
voice. "Then you love your life more than you do me?"

"No, no," he stammered, "I am ready to die!"

Adele rose quickly, filled a cut-glass goblet with a
brown fluid, which she took out of a small ebony box,
and gave it to her adorer, whom she had condemned
to death.

"To your health, Adele," he cried, with the enthusiasm of despair, and emptied it at a draught, still
kneeling before the cruel beauty, whilst she looked
at him with strange curiosity, and her bosom heaved
with indescribable emotion.

"Give me your hand, your dear hand," the Russian
murmured; "my senses are failing me." She drew him
to her bosom, his head drooped and he was wrapped
in darkness . . .

Two hours later he opened his eyes. He was still
lying at Adele's feet, who had rested his head on her
lap, and was looking down at him with a happy smile.

"What is the matter with me?" he asked, getting
up

"Warndorf!" the lovely woman said tenderly.

"Am I dreaming? I did not die?" he said, looking at
Adele in astonishment

"No, no, you are alive, and for the future you shall live for me, as my lover, my husband!" she replied; "for I love you as you love me, more than my life."

"And that brown draught—the poison?"

"Was an opiate."

"What for?"

"A test." Warndorf rose hastily.

"Adele," he exclaimed, "you say that you love me, and yet you could be capable of letting me experience all the tortures of mortal terror, for the sake of your own amusement? No, the test was too cruel, and a woman who can act like that, cannot possibly have my heart, and, above all, she has not that becoming seriousness, which alone ennobles a woman and her love."

"Warndorf," she stammered, "what has come to you all of a sudden? Do you not love me any longer?"

"No, Baroness, I do not love you any longer and I can never love you again!" Warndorf said, in a firm and manly voice; "you have played with me much too frivolously, Farewell!"

"For Heaven's sake, do you intend to make me wretched?" she cried, throwing her arms around him.

"You have made us both unhappy," the Russian replied. "Goodbye." And with these words, he extricated himself from her grasp, and it was in vain that she threw herself at his feet; he showed himself strong, and went away in spite of all.

When her lady's maid came into the room, she found her lying on the floor, insensible.

ON THE MOUNTAIN OF VENUS

NOT very long ago, I made the acquaintance of a painter in Vienna, quite accidentally, and yet not unintentionally on my part.

For months we had been in the habit of drinking our cup of afternoon coffee at the same table and of reading our newspapers, sitting back to back. The pale young man with the short, curly hair, and with large, melancholy, bright, black eyes, attracted me, and the sad touch of fatalism in his face, which was almost beautiful, interested me particularly. He seemed to me, to be one of those persons who carry their own misfortunes and fate in their breast, and who have given up the fight against them in silent resignation.

A very peculiar picture in the *Fliegende Blätter* brought about our acquaintance; it represented a hideous female ape in the well-known attitude of the figure of Justice, beneath which was written: *The original of Karl Vogt's Venus de Medici.*

As much as the picture offended my taste and my feelings, I could not help laughing at it, which attracted my neighbour's attention, so I put the paper down before him; he seized it quickly, glanced at it, and then threw it down again, just as quickly.

"How can you laugh at such a thing?" he said, almost angrily.

"No doubt it is shameful, but it is very funny."

"I cannot laugh at anything that is sacred for me," he said. "Let them caricature everything which human folly has surrounded with a halo, but not love, which is the holiest object we have, and woman, who is the symbol of mankind, and the mystery of our existence."

That was how we became acquainted, and soon, intimate.

Before long, he invited me to go and see him in his studio, or perhaps I ought to say, in the garret where his easel stood, and in which two half-finished pictures were hanging.

"Today, you shall see another Venus," he said, after he had looked through his portfolios and sketches. He locked the door, opened a cupboard and took out a canvas, which he half turned away from me and put carefully on to the easel, and then remained standing before it, so absorbed in looking at it, that he appeared to have quite forgotten the world and me.

"A Venus?" I asked, in order to wake him out of his dream. He started, looked at me as if he were not quite in his senses, and at last smiled. Then he beckoned to me to stand before the picture, and when I had done so, I was dumb. The scene, which stood out of the canvas in bold outline and splendid colouring, seemed to assume life as I looked at it, and I began to feel something akin to terror at the sight of the devilishly beautiful woman, who was sitting up in bed in order again to bewitch the man she loved, and again to ensnare him with her soft, golden locks; I was frightened to the depths of my soul at that wonderful, classic, shape, at those soft, devouring, dark eyes, which flashed from under their half-closed lids, at that small, half-open mouth, with its small, white teeth, at that victorious smile that hovered round it, and I myself seemed to feel the soft noose of silky hair, with which she was threatening to strangle the Tannhäuser, round my neck.

"Such a picture," I said at last, "nobody could paint who had not been to Venus' mountain himself."

The pale painter nodded.

"I have been there myself, and I painted it there," he replied, sadly; "that picture is mine, and no one else shall have it. I would not part with it for the world!"

He took it down hastily and locked it up again.

"Do you know her?" he said, after a short pause.

"No," I replied. "Is she a real living woman?"

Instead of replying, he opened a large photographic album and handed it to me. It was the same, beautiful, light-haired woman of his picture, but in a white summer dress, and with a straw hat with roses in it, in her hand.

"So it is a secret," I said.

"As you please," my friend replied; "secret, and yet no secret, for the lady is not one of those who shun publicity."

"What do you mean?"

"I mean that I may as well tell you the strange story of this picture."

"I am all curiosity to hear it."

"Very well."

He sat down on his bed, and looked straight before him like a man who is talking in a delirium.

"The idea for that picture was in my mind for a long time, like a hidden germ that must come to light.

"It formed part of my nature; it was my fate which first of all made it strike me in the mist of imagination; and it was my fate which drove me to it, and embedded itself in it. I drew the outline, and then sought for a model for the goddess of love. You know what a model is, but you will scarcely know how difficult it is to find a beautiful model, even in Vienna, where the women of all ranks are particularly beautiful, and all the types of loveliness are plentiful, on account of the various races which are represented in that capital, and also on account of the great crossing of various races. But a bad woman, as a rule, makes a bad model. Do not take that for a mere idealistic notion. Now in Vienna there are some perfectly virtuous girls who are artists' models, in order that they may be able to support their old parents, and respectable, married women, who prefer to expose their beauty, from love for their husband and children, to their virtue.

"I therefore searched for one amongst them, and I offered any price, but I could not find what I wanted. I had made up my mind that my Venus must have light hair and dark eyes, and at length I took the unusual course of advertising in the newspapers.

"For some time I made no reply, but, at last, I received a letter, which was as peculiar in its style as my advertisement had been, and was as follows:

"'A young, beautiful lady, with light hair and dark eyes, will be your model for the goddess of love, but you must look upon it as a favour which your Venus bestows on you, and neither ask her who she is, nor make enquiries about her. And woe to you, if you are ungrateful enough to play the traitor, when you are approached in the fullest confidence! You will be expected next Saturday night at Eleven o'clock, at the rotunda in the Prater.'"

"And did you accept the invitation?"

"How can you ask me such a question? Yes, I went with a beating heart. It was a stormy winter's night; a carriage was waiting for me, and an old footman, in a livery which I did not recognise, helped me in, got in after me, and sat down by my side, bandaged my eyes, and we drove off.

"Evidently, the coachman was intentionally driving hither and thither in order to puzzle me, for it was fully an hour before we arrived at our destination. I was requested to get out in the covered gateway of a large house, and the old footman, who now took the bandage off my eyes, showed me up a flight of stairs, on which pots of flowers stood, and then left me alone in a brilliantly lighted and well-warmed drawing-room, that was most luxuriously furnished. But not for long.

"The curtain which covered the door rustled, a long, flowing silk train joined in that melodious rustle, and a woman, the goddess of love herself, stood before me!

"But why should I describe her? I have painted her, and so you know her. Picture to yourself my Venus, who captures Tannhäuser with her curls, only concealed by a dark dress, with the golden waves of her hair flowing down her back, and with a half curious and half mocking smile on her lips.

"She gave me one single look out of her demonic eyes, only one look, and I was ensnared, bewitched, and not until she put the roguish question:

"'Am I beautiful enough for you?' she let her garments fall, and suddenly stood before me like the goddess of love herself, and I . . . .

"When I look into myself, into my soul, I still see that devilish woman standing before me as she stood then—but then, I was lying before her on my knees, and kissing her small, bare feet.

"She kept me with her, as an inmate of her house, or rather as her prisoner. I was not allowed to ask her name, or to leave my room unless she sent for me. I painted her and loved her, and she—allowed herself to be painted and loved.

"She had not forbidden me to think about her, and when I was alone, my thoughts were constantly occupied with her. I took her for a lady, who had thrown herself into my arms from a freak; perhaps she was a Russian; at any rate, her harsh German pointed that way. She was rich, wonderfully rich, as could be seen from the minutest article in the house, and from her expensive and tasteful dresses, which she was continually renewing.

"I had finished my painting, and given her a copy of it, but still she would not tell me who she was, or let me go. And I—at last loved her so madly, that I could no longer imagine how I could live without her.

"'You are mine,' I said to her once, 'and I want to possess you altogether and forever.'

"'That is impossible,' she replied, growing pale.

"'So you will not consent?'

"'I cannot.'

"I laughed aloud.

"You cannot?'

"'Well then, I must make up my mind to separate from you.'

"'But listen to me; I love you, alone,' she cried in agony, 'but I cannot belong to you.'

"'So you are the wife of another man?'

"'No . . .'

"'What then?'

"'His mistress.'

"I looked at her, feeling utterly crushed. 'His mistress!' I murmured. 'Woman, what have I done to you that you have made me so wretched, so terribly wretched, just in order to help you to while away an hour or two?'

"'Oh I have known you for a long time and I love you; that is my crime, and that only.'

"I made my escape that same night, but since then I have had no rest, and no happy moment; I cannot paint now, for the goddess of love pursues me with her dark eyes, she throws out the snares of her golden hair at me, and I must return with her to the Mountain of Venus, and then my dry maul-stick will flourish again, and perhaps bear blooming roses again."

THE STORY OF
THE PERPETUAL STUDENT

FLIES hummed on the dingy window panes and pens scratched away across paper. The assistant professor hummed—he lectured today for the first time in the professor's place; the bluish-yellow spirit flame hummed, as it burned under the retort on the lecturer's table; and, when the pens ceased scratching, the students hummed also, making use of the pause to read, half aloud, what they had written.

Notwithstanding this Sabbath stillness, but little attention or zeal prevailed in the large lecture hall. The assistant observed this, as did also the man who was crowded into the furthest corner of the last bench and who listened to his words with honest reverence. The student's eyes were fastened on the speaker's face, with an expression of mingled astonishment and despair, and each individual hair on his head seemed to stand on end in sympathy.

This head, already turned perceptibly grey, appeared a little strange among the fresh, almost child-like faces of the other hearers, with their clustering locks of rich brown or blond hair.

When the lecture was at an end, the figure to which the head belonged stood up in the class in all its height and breadth, like a century-old oak in the midst of tender sprouts.

"Who is that gentleman in the brown coat," asked the assistant of the janitor. The latter smiled.

"He is no gentleman," he replied, "but the 'Perpetual Student'. He is so called by everyone. His name is really Nikodem Rawa. He is nearly forty years old, and he has now certainly been as much as ten years in the junior class."

Old Mr. Rawa, Nikodem's father, was an unadulterated Little Russian, neither diluted nor sweetened, a blacksmith in a suburb of Lemberg. His pale-green son, who had shot up tall and narrow chested, showed little inclination toward this noisy occupation. He liked to sit in a quiet nook, with his mother's prayer-book in his hand, as if reading. When he was finally asked, in real earnest, what he would like to become, he shyly declared that he wished to attend school, so that he might learn to know all the works of God in heaven and on earth.

His father, who did not know a letter, and who kept his accounts with marks instead of figures, agreed at once; not so the mother and other relatives, who perceived a wicked innovation in little Nikodem's resolution.

Whereat, the smith exclaimed, placing his son in the middle of the room:

"How can these poor little hands swing a hammer? Have pity!"

And they all pitied him, and that self-same day he came in possession of a reading book, a catechism, and a slate, and began, at ten years of age, to attend the normal school.

Learning agreed so well with the little fellow that he began at once to develop most vigorously in height and breadth, while his large hands and feet promised a still more thrifty growth.

His mind, however, did not in any degree keep pace with his body. His ability was as small as his yearning after knowledge was great and pathetic. It was a resigned, patient, never-tiring soul that dwelt in this gladiator's frame, but a soul of pitiful poverty and helplessness.

And yet Nikodem passed successfully through the preparatory school; for, as he continued to grow and grow, to everybody's terror, so he also studied without ceasing, day and night.

To be sure, he remained in each class two years, and in the last class of the preparatory school three years, even. Yet, the day came when he was permitted to carry a cane and the professors addressed him with the prefix "Mr." And, though he had only attained the dignity of a junior at twenty-six, it still served to increase his satisfaction and pride. To a lame person ascending a high mountain, the view that the summit offers seems, doubtless, much more glorious than to one who ascends lightly and rapidly on sound limbs.

To Nikodem's mind, it seemed now as if the seals of learning were about to be unclasped. He opened his eyes wide, as if by this means to pierce the obscurity, and listened to the professors as though possessed of a hundred ears, instead of two. But the darkness remained impenetrable, and what he heard was only empty sound.

He worried himself frightfully, but without any result whatever. Anxious, stubborn, restless, he inspired all, professors and students, with compassion. He perspired over his pamphlets, took walks with them, and even ate his meals with a spoon or a fork in one hand and a book in the other. He conversed with his books as with living, reasoning beings; he demanded explanations of them, caressed them, quarrelled with them, and cursed them; he implored, conjured them, earnestly, with tears; and yet, for him, they remained dumb.

Whether he spent whole nights studying aloud by his little lamp; or whether he flung logarithms and Atlantes behind the stove, it amounted to the same thing.

Nikodem simply did not comprehend what he was about. A bandage lay over his eyes. He did not progress a step, not half a step, and after he had twice tried and failed to pass the examinations, he remained ever after fixed in the class.

"I cannot shoe hoofs, I cannot plough the fields," he said one day to his father, resigned to his fate; "so I must study, even though I make no progress. I must, but henceforth I will maintain myself."

The elder only laughed.

"To study is your affair," he said; "but to support you is mine. Where so many eat, you also may be filled."

But Nikodem's upright nature rebelled. He began to give lessons, to copy for the professors, and to write parts for the theatre.

He moved quietly one evening into a little room near the manager of the theatre, and took his meals at a Jewish restaurant in the Serwaniza, the Ghetto of Lemberg. He gave up trying to pass the examinations for a third time, and he also gave up further study.

But it seemed impossible for him to say farewell forever to the recitation bench and the large blackboard. He continued a student. The professors tolerated him willingly, as a sort of shining example of industry to the others, and the students treated him as an heirloom lovingly received from their predecessors, and sorrowfully turned him over to their successors.

They called him, jestingly, the "Perpetual Student"; yet, for all that, they loved him none the less. Everybody loved him; it would have been difficult to hate him. Where was there another so sociable, so good-natured, so without deceit, and, at the same time, so enthusiastic for all that is great, and true, and beautiful, as was Nikodem Rawa?

He never missed a lecture. Why should he, when the vacations appeared in his eyes only a necessary evil, to which he resigned himself year after year with a sigh? He was wholly at a loss to understand how anyone, while the voice of the professor resounded from the vaulted roof in exalted monotone, could occupy himself with anything else than the subject of the discourse; how anyone could yawn.

And now, these young philosophers, who heard for the first time what he had so often heard, allowed themselves, from year to year, certain frivolous jokes with their instructors, in whom everything appeared venerable to him—not their learning, not their voices alone, but their coughing, their hawking, their large spectacles, and even the snuff box, out of which they took their pinches of snuff.

Nikodem knew beforehand what would come, must come. He was no less certain that Augustus followed Julius Caesar than he was that there would be drumming with canes at the first reading of the roll-register, and that at the so-called "Asses' bridge," in geometry, there would be an outburst of resounding laughter.

It was, likewise, a matter of course that the favourite among the students, Schwabe Maus, should, each year at his first lecture on universal history, find a dead mouse on his desk, that he should every time remove it with unruffled severity, saying:

"My name is Maus, and I throw the mouse out of the window."

Nothing surprised him, and yet his mind was continually under tension, and not seldom profoundly moved, when the old gentlemen, with their shining crowns and white neckties, expounded, with the beautiful enthusiasm of youth, the great deeds of the Romans, the glorious propositions of ethics, or the wonderful discoveries of science, to their youthful auditors.

Nikodem deported himself among his colleagues as he did in the lecture hall. He was content to be with them. If they went out to the shore, or the sand mountain, or were together in the room of a friend, and they began a debate, he would be happy only to sit quietly in some corner and listen to them. But seldom did an exclamation escape him, such as "You don't say so!" or, "How is that?"

Still more seldom did he betray himself by an asserting nod of the head. Only when someone began to declaim a poem or a scene from *Faust*, without that consecrating stillness which his heart demanded, did it happen that Nikodem allowed himself to be carried away so far as to say:

"Attention there, you young people!"

Or, if someone composed a couple of stanzas, it appeared inadmissible to Nikodem to make any investigation as to whether they were good or not, he would tolerate no censure. He moved uneasily on his chair, shook his head, gesticulated with his hands; and, finally, most likely, jumped to his feet, clasped the poet in his arms, and kissed him.

On the whole, Nikodem was heartily glad that he had been led within the student circles, and expressed his overflowing thankfulness by a hundred little services to his colleagues. So he became, in time, the indispensable factotum of the undergraduates, beloved by all.

A faithful elephant in every intrigue, in every excursion an unwearied pack animal, he was, at the same time, tailor, shoemaker, dyer, and seamstress. He also performed as eagerly the duty of a speaking tube or a pump. He was an artist, in that he could restore worn-out boots, so that one might appear in any drawing-room with them. He could also transform an old or a soiled coat into a new one by means of thread, ink, and soap.

Who can count the wakeful nights he spent by the side of the sick! Who the number of money lenders with whom he was in active business relations! There was nothing that Nikodem did not know how to convert into money by means of one or another of his curly-headed, bearded friends. And so every student who had anything to pawn or to sell naturally made him his confident. In raising money, the "Perpetual Student" was a downright genius.

With this object in view, he frequently visited the excellent Schmol Herschel, whom he never annoyed with old garments or with a watch that would not go.

Schmol Herschel never demanded a bond, or even a note. He lent money only to "safe" people, but to these on their bare word. To him, safe people were not those who passed for rich, but whose faces pleased him; and, as Schmol Herschel was an excellent judge of men and a good business man, only honest faces pleased him, and he never made a mistake.

Nikodem Rawa had such a face, and Schmol Herschel would, in a case of necessity, have bet ten thousand florins on that face.

Nikodem stood, moreover, in high favour with the pretty and portly Madam Herschel, whom he now and then brought a forbidden book, and who liked to discuss literature and the theatre with him.

When Nikodem came to Schmol Herschel, he would first speak of everything else, and then of money; but Herschel, on the other hand, liked best to speak about money first, and then of everything else; and so, on each occasion, a generous contest would arise between the two.

"I have brought you something," began Nikodem, "perhaps, you cannot guess what it is, Mrs. Herschel."

"Do you want money?" whispered Schmol to him, with his usual amiability.

"Can you guess, then, Mr. Herschel?" continued Nikodem, producing a book.

"How can I guess? Am I a junior, like you?" exclaimed Schmol, adding softly, almost tenderly. "Whom do you want money for?"

Nikodem lifted the cover of the book and handed it to Mrs. Herschel, who fairly burst through her fur jacket with satisfaction.

"Heine's *Traveling Sketches*!"

"Yes, Heine's *Traveling Sketches*."

"You ought surely to be set in gold, dear Mr. Rawa," responded the lady in flute-like tones, while she allowed an expression of fondness to play in her eyes.

"So, here are fifty florins," cried Schmol Herschel, thrusting them into Nikodem's pocket; "or, do you need more?"

"I need only thirty for the lawyer Glinski. His father has an estate in the Tarnopol region——"

"Have I asked you about that?"

Schmol Herschel interrupted him with an injured air.

"I have not asked you. If I give the money to you, what need have I to know whether Mr. Glinski has a father, or whether the father has an estate or no estate? You will return me my fifty florins, and I want to know nothing more."

All this, and much besides, came into his simple, modest life like light and colour. How happy he was when, of an evening, the students met with this one or that one, smoked, drank beer, and sang student songs—things strongly forbidden in those days. Then an exalted feeling possessed him, as if he had taken part in the conspiracy against Julius Caesar, and he sang, probably, the "Gaudeamus" on his way home, beating time with his large student cane on the flagstones.

The poorly-furnished room that he occupied near the manager of the theatre, in the third story of the theatre itself, enclosed no inconsiderable part of his happiness.

To be sure, he enjoyed here only a wonderful view of roofs and stairs, lines with drying clothes, carpets that gave out clouds of dust under Spanish canes, and wood piled up in the backyards; but, as an offset to this, he had sometimes, also, a glimpse of a strip of blue sky, and, year after year, swallows built their cosy nests under his window.

The furniture of the room consisted of a problematical bed, a dreadful table, and one chair that always afforded him an opportunity of applying practically the laws of equilibrium. As his whole wardrobe had place on a nail in the wall, what use had he for a chest? And what purpose could a second chair have served, when his box, covered with a red cloth, offered both a convenient and a showy seat? This box was, at the same time, his dressing table, his hearth, upon which he boiled his tea every evening, and his pantry.

The door of his little room was so low that he was compelled to stoop every time he came in or went out, and the ceiling was just high enough to prevent his striking his head against it.

As amends for these inconveniences, the walls were pasted over from top to bottom with coloured prints taken from the theatrical papers of Vienna, so that his eyes could, at any time, refresh themselves with scenes from the latest operas and plays.

Half a dozen unwashed and uncombed children cried and stormed in his neighbourhood, from morning till evening; but, as a compensation for this, he also heard, from time to time, the tones of the theatre orchestra floating upward when there was a rehearsal below; and, when there was nothing else, he heard the bass drum, whose hollow resonance seemed to him like heavenly music. And many a time he saw the employees of the theatre bring out the decorations from the store-room, and he rejoiced over the trees, the rocks, the well-springs and the gorgeous canopy.

The kitchen fire sometimes smoked viciously, and the smoke had the odious habit of penetrating his little room through gaping slits in the door; but nobody hindered him from opening the window, and if he wished to do more, he could thrust his head out and have the rare pleasure of overlooking, as from a balloon, the theatrical people, who dwelt mostly in the theatre buildings.

He had, for instance, shed tears during the presentation of *Don Carlos*; then, how comforting it was for him to see Posa, on the next day, smoking a pipe, King Philip rock his crying child, or Epoli mending her husband's socks.

Nikodem took his breakfast with the people of the house. The coffee looked, perhaps, like soapsuds and tasted like a mixture of lamp oil and slacked lime; but, in compensation, what gossip could not the manager retail about theatrical people, especially the ladies!

It was as in a droll fairy play, when the veils before the cloud scene are raised, one after another, until, at last, the beautiful fairy becomes visible behind transparent gauze. Nikodem listened almost as reverently as in the auditorium, and the little theatrical secrets that he knew served to enhance his esteem with Schmol Herschel, and his popularity among the students.

In the meantime, the evening brought him his hours of relaxation. Then no cooking was going on; there was no smoke; neither was there any noise, for the children were asleep. Then he would sit in his old dressing-gown, with the long Turkish pipe on the table, lost in some good book, or copying, with innocent joy and breathless suspense, some treatise for one of the professors or a part out of a play.

Quiet as it was, he was, nevertheless, not alone. He loved animals, and would only too gladly have had a dog, or at least a bird, with him; but, as this was too expensive, he contented himself with a spider that had set up her airy tent directly above his desk, and the mice that dwelt beneath the floor. When he was writing, the spider liked to let himself down and swing over the paper by a long thread, or even run hither and thither over the same; and the mice promenaded about the bedstead, or industriously trimmed their velvety coats, or seized the crumbs he threw to them, devouring them leisurely, as they held them daintily between their little paws.

The most hallowed hours were those that Nikodem spent with his father. When he sat with the honest, sensible old gentleman in the large, tidy sitting-room, then neither of them had another wish, none ever so small. His father was the only person in the world whom Nikodem impressed with his learning, who honestly admired him.

How could this homage other than do him good, him who, all his life long, everywhere, was accustomed to stand in shadows? Here the sunshine fell upon him full and warm, and it came from the best heart in the world, his father's heart. Nikodem told him what was in the papers; whatever happened in the world that was weighty and wonderful; explained this and that to him; what there was interesting the minds of men; the new inventions and discoveries; and never grew weary of answering his father's questions. All this he did modestly and lovingly, without a trace of assumption.

How the eyes of the honest Russian smith shone when his son had left him. With what pride he remarked to his friends and relations:

"There is a head for you, and how he can talk! One always learns something from him."

And the thoughts of Nikodem were no less good and friendly, when he left the elder Rawa.

"If I had studied only to give my father pleasure," he thought, "it would have been worth all the trouble."

Nikodem occasionally received a pass to the theatre from the manager. He ascended the steep stairs leading to the highest gallery, each time with an emotion largely made up of devout awe. He never went to objectionable plays; seldom to an opera. When he

took his place on the narrow wooden bench immediately before the parapet, there was surely a great, a
soul-stirring poem to be presented. The time that he
spent here waiting in quietness and obscurity until
the rising of the curtain had something consecrating in it, whether he now listened while the other
students whistled snatches from the latest pieces or
discussed the performances of the actors, or whether
he, undisturbed, gave himself wholly to the pleasing
sensation of expectancy.

While the play was going on below him, he con-
ducted himself only a little differently from a child.
He laughed, he cried, he was angered, struck with
terror; his heart leaped with joy and he never thought
of applauding. What he saw and heard was for him no
make-believe, but living reality.

His ideal was Madam Lomnizka, a no longer
young, but talented and experienced, actress, who,
thanks to the favour of the public and the protection
of the management, played all the leading parts; the
perverse little kitten, as well as the blood-stained Lady
Macbeth, or the unfortunate Scotch Mary, Nikodem
felt a sort of adoration for this woman. He held his
breath when she stepped upon the boards. The rustling of the train made him tremble. The sound of her
voice dominated him completely. Its every tone found
an echo in his heart. He became tender, passionate,
bold, exalted, wild or sorrowful; nay, even deceitful
and blood-thirsty, under its influence.

How happy he became once to see her wardrobe
hung out for an airing in the corridor of the first story, where she lived—the blood-red robe of ermine in

which she wrapped herself as Barbara Radziwil, the white nightgown of Desdemona, the coat of mail of the Maid of Orleans.

Daily, at breakfast, he inquired fully of the manager about Madam Lomnizka. All that concerned her seemed to him to be of importance and interest, even what she ate and drank, and at what hour she arose in the morning.

"Oh, if I could but once, one single time, come near her," he exclaimed one day, "I would give ten years of my life for the privilege!"

"Why give ten years of your life away?" asked the manager. "Give me a twenty and you shall enjoy this happiness a whole evening."

The bargain was closed, and the following evening the manager took Nikodem upon the stage and dressed him in wide pantaloons, doublet, and high boots. He clapped a cap on his head and buckled a sword to his side. "Who am I then?" asked the student timidly.

"You are an attendant of the Count von Croix and have to hand this letter to the Duchess of Burgundy, Madam Lomnizka, in the third act."

Nikodem concealed the letter on his person and hid himself behind one of the side doors. By and by the actors, costumed and rouged, appeared upon the stage, and there carried on their accustomed jesting. Finally, came also the rustling of the train of the Duchess of Burgundy, and Madam Lomnizka stepped to the curtain in order to get a glimpse of the public.

At the sight of her, Nikodem was seized by a nameless anguish, but her tall figure, elastic step, her bosom, encircled by the swelling ermine, and now, especially, her face, with the great shining eyes, put him more and more into a sort of intoxicated condition and inspired him with a wonderfully bold thought.

He took out his theatrical letter, and saw that it contained a blank sheet. Quickly resolved, he wrote upon it a short, but glowing, tribute, and again concealed the fantastic document in his yellow doublet.

The third act came. Nikodem stood at the door, pressing his hand to his heart, as Madam Lomnizka stretched herself divinely on the convenient couch. Now the manager gave him the signal. With extravagant earnestness, Nikodem hemmed, as though he had to speak Hamlet's soliloquy, entered with quiet dignity, knelt before her on one knee, and handed the letter to the wondrous woman.

Madam Lomnizka opened the missive and glanced at it mechanically, and then, quickly and searchingly, at the man at her feet, only finally to speak, with an emotion of tempered dignity, the words:

"Tell the count that I await him."

Nikodem arose, bowed reverently, and withdrew with firm steps. He had learned this kind of gait by watching the great stage heroes.

Madam Lomnizka had put his lines in her bosom, under the swelling ermine. She read them in the dressing-room, and, at the beginning of the fourth act, she asked the manager:

"Who is the young man who handed me the letter?"

"A student," the manager replied, as he discreetly took a pinch of snuff. "A young man of good family, who cherishes an almost insane enthusiasm for you. He wished to enjoy the happiness of only once coming into your presence,"—the old fox made a courtesy— "and so I have made him happy."

Madam Lomnizka smiled.

In the last act occurred a soliloquy, during which she had to look toward the sinking sun. She leaned against the window. There, to her and to his own no little astonishment, stood Nikodem. Not dead, not living, he would gladly have disappeared; but his feet were glued to the spot, and the sweat of anguish stood on his brow.

But what was that? Between the quavering words, spoken with pathos, there sounded from angel lips:

"Wait for me after the performance."

Then, all of a sudden, wings grew on the soles of poor Nikodem's feet. He flew to his wardrobe, changed his clothes with a rush, and, as the curtain fell, he stood ready in the dim passage leading to the stage. He stood a long time before a tall female form, wrapped in a long fur robe that revealed itself by the feeble light of a dying flame, and summoned him, with a condescending nod of the head, to accompany it.

Nikodem dared not offer her his arm, not even to walk by her side. He followed her through the passages and up the steps to the first floor, like a lackey, always two respectful paces behind her.

When they reached her little salon, he saw a thousand golden flies dancing before his eyes, and his whole body trembled, so that the robe which Madam Lomnizka threw off with a majestic movement, slipped from his hands to the floor. They seated themselves and the actress spoke of the rare pleasure he had prepared for her in enabling her to know such a sincere friend of art. She assured him that she loved nothing better than to chat, after the representation, with a gifted man about the piece and her part.

Madam Lomnizka led the conversation further, while his whole vocabulary on that evening consisted of the words "yes," "no," and "wonderful." When he went away, he stumbled three times, first, as he kissed her hand, then over the doorstep, and once more while descending the steps.

Two days later, Madam Lomnizka played Phædra, and sent Nikodem a ticket for a reserved seat. He was beside himself with joy; but the nearer the hour for the performance approached, the more uneasy he became, and when he finally found himself seated in the theatre between an officer and a richly-dressed lady, he was in a truly uncomfortable, even dismal, state of mind. Whether he looked to the right, to the left, or straight before him, he had ever the impression that all eyes, all opera-glasses, were directed only upon him. He resolved never to descend again from his gallery to this dangerous place. He remained ever afterward true to his resolution.

Madam Lomnizka soon became aware of the actual state of things regarding her fanatical adorer. She felt that she could never step down from the pedestal in his presence, and so always kept him at a certain moral distance.

Strictly considered, this was quite unnecessary. He worshipped her, loved her to ecstasy, he deified her;

but he was contented merely to come into her presence; happy when permitted to take a cup of tea with her; blessed if her glance at any time strayed from the stage up to him in the gallery. No word betraying his feelings for her ever escaped him. Never did he dare so much as to touch the ends of her fingers.

At the same time, he appeared to be totally blind, and to his own advantage. Would he, perchance, have been happier had he seen that this woman, who, in her fur wrapping, could sink so bewitchingly into the silk cushions, was quite past her bloom; that her cheeks and lips were painted, and her teeth false? Would it, perhaps, have been agreeable to him to discover that Madam Lomnizka was made up of the most frightful grimaces? Certainly not. These grimaces impressed him, even transported him with ecstasy.

If now the light annoyed her eyes and he hurriedly drew the curtain; if the heat became suddenly unbearable and she ordered the window raised, only to have it closed again the next instant, and allowed herself to be wrapped by him in her great fur robe and all the bear and wolf skins that were at hand; or, if she felt such an irresistible longing after a pineapple that he sped through the whole city to find her one—all this only served to make her appear more unusual, interesting, and lovely in his eyes. If he had run about all day doing errands for her, and came to her in the evening, tired, wet to the skin, and possibly hungry, she had only to deliver up her beautiful little hand, for a few moments, to his hot kisses, and he was fully compensated.

She ever maintained her exalted, godlike character, and, indeed, when she wished to be amiable, she showed herself only gracious and condescending. But that was sufficient for this poor, modest, helpless man. He would have been happy, if she had never smiled upon him.

Madam Lomnizka made use of Nikodem in various ways. Now, she used him to overhear her rehearsal or to wind her watch; now, to bring about the applause that was her due, as well as to throw her bouquets and garlands, and, on proper occasions, to give her a serenade. She used him, also, industriously as "a voice of the public," and to pummel the critics.

And whatever the world might say of her, Nikodem remained always her steadfast friend. All that he asked was to be allowed to love, to adore her; and, as his love continued ever unassuming, and his worship never became burdensome, why should not Madam Lomnizka have tolerated him?

She did always tolerate him at her feet, as the professors had tolerated him in the furthest corner of the lecture hall, and also the students, as a sort of familiar spirit.

There are human beings who, all their lives long, are simply endured. They are only happy when they are so endured; and such a being was Nikodem Rawa.

THE EXILE

I SHALL not tell you the name of the place nor of the man. It was very far from here, on a hot and fertile part of the coast. Since the morning we had been following the shore that was covered with the crops, and the blue sea which was dazzling, under the rays of the sun. Flowers grew in close proximity to the waves, small, soft, rippling waves. It was a hot day, with that soft perfumed heat which rises from rich, moist and fertile soil, and one felt almost as if one were inhaling germs of life.

I was told that at night I should find hospitality in the house of the Frenchman who lived in the middle of an orange grove, at the extremity of the promontory. I did not know who he was. He had arrived one morning ten years previously, had bought some land, planted vineyards and sown corn, and had worked furiously. And then, month by month, year by, year he had enlarged his domain, continually fertilizing the virgin soil, and had thus amassed a fortune by his indefatigable labour.

But people said that he went on working. He rose at daybreak, and was in the fields until night, overlooking everything himself, for he appeared harassed by one fixed idea, tormented by the insatiable desire for money which nothing can appease; but now he seemed to be very rich.

The sun was setting when I reached his house which stood, as I have said, on the extremity of a cape in the midst of orange trees. It was a plain, square house overlooking the sea.

As I went up to it, a man with a long beard came to the door, and after having saluted him, I begged for shelter for the night, whereupon he gave me his hand with a smile:

"Come in, Monsieur," he said; "you are at home here."

He showed me a room, placed a man-servant at my disposal with the perfect ease and good breeding of a man of the world, and as he left me he said:

"We shall have dinner as you come down."

We dined alone, on a terrace overlooking the sea. At first I talked to him about that rich, distant, unknown country, and he smiled and replied absently:

"Yes, it is a beautiful country, but no country can please you, when you are far from the native-land which you love."

"You regret France, then?"

"I regret Paris."

"Why do you not return then?"

"Oh! I shall go back."

And gradually, we began to talk about French, society, the boulevards and Paris generally. He questioned me like a man who used to know it well, and mentioned many names to me, those names which are familiar on the pavement near the Vaudeville Theatre.

"Whom does one meet at Tortoni's now?"

"Always the same people, except those who are now dead."

I looked at him closely, as I was haunted by some old recollection. I had certainly seen him somewhere before! But where and when? He appeared tired, although he looked vigorous, sad, though resolute. His long, fair beard descended on his breast, and at times he took hold of it close to his chin and passed his hand down it. He was rather bald, with thick eyebrows and a heavy moustache which mingled with the hair on his cheeks.

The sun was sinking into the sea behind us, and throwing its rays on the shore. The orange trees, which were in bloom, exhaled their strong, delicious perfume with the evening air. He seemed to see nothing but me, and looking at me intently, he appeared to perceive that distant, beloved and well-known picture of the wide, shady pavement, which extends from the Madeleine to the Rue Drouot.

"Do you know Boutrelle?"

"Certainly I do."

"Has he altered very much?"

"Yes, he has turned quite white."

"And La Ridamie?"

"He is just the same."

"And the women? Tell me about the women. Do you know Suzanne Verner?"

"Yes, she is very stout; done for."

"Ah! and Sophie Astier?"

"Dead."

"Poor girl! Is . . . Do you know . . ."

But he stopped abruptly, and then in an altered voice, and with his face suddenly grown pale, he continued:

"No, I had better not speak about it any more, it only pains me."

And he got up, as if to change the current of his thoughts, and asking me whether I should like to go indoors, he went before me into the house.

The downstairs rooms were enormous, bare, and melancholy, and looked as if they were never used. Plates and glasses were scattered about the tables, left there by dark-skinned servants, who were continually moving about in the vast house. Two guns hung on nails against the wall, and in the corners there were fishing-rods, spades, dried palm leaves, objects of all kinds laid down at haphazard when he came in, and which were within reach when he went out.

My host smiled. "It is the house, or rather the hovel, of an exile," he said, "but my room is more tidy. Let us go there."

When I got into it, I almost could have fancied that I was in a second-hand dealer's shop, for it was full of those incongruous, strange and varied objects which one feels sure are mementos. On the walls there were two good pictures by well-known artists, stuffs, arms, swords and pistols, and just in the middle of the longest panel, there was a square of white satin framed in gold. I went to look at in some surprise, and noticed a hair pin sticking in the middle of the shining material, and my host laid his hand upon my shoulder: "That," he said, "is the only thing which I look at here, and the only one which I have seen for ten years. Monsieur Prudhomme declared: 'This sword is the proudest day of my life,' and I can say: 'That this pin is my whole life.'"

I tried to find something commonplace to say, and observed: "You have suffered on account of a woman."

"Say that I am suffering like a wretched man. But come onto my balcony. Just now a name rose to my lips, which I did not venture to pronounce, for if you had replied *dead*, as you did when I spoke of Sophie Astier, I should have blown out my brains this very day."

We went out to a large balcony, from which one could see two bays, one on the right and the other on the left, enclosed by high, grey mountains. The sun had disappeared and only lit up the earth by the reflections from the sky, and he went on:

"Is Jeanne de Limours alive still?

He gazed at me fixedly, with a look of anguish in his eyes, but I smiled and replied:

"Yes, by Jove . . . and prettier than ever."

"Do you know her?"

"Yes."

He hesitated for a moment and continued:

"Very intimately . . ."

"No."

Then he took my hand and said: "Tell me about her."

"But there is nothing to tell; she is one of the most charming women, or rather girls, in Paris, and the most talked about. She leads an agreeable and prince-ly life, that is all."

"I love her," he murmured, as if he had said: "I am going to die," and then suddenly he went on: "Ah for three years ours was a terrible and delicious existence. I nearly killed her five or six times, and she tried to tear out my eyes with that pin which you have just seen. Look at that little white mark under my left eye. We loved each other! How could I explain that passion? You would not understand it. There must be such a thing as simple love, made up of the double impulse of two minds and two souls; but assuredly there exists a fierce love, which tortures us cruelly, made up of the invincible linking together of two dissimilar beings, who at once detest and adore one another.

"That girl ruined me in three years. I had four million francs which she got through with that sweet smile which seemed to fall from her eyes to her lips. You know her? There is something irresistible about her! What is it? I cannot tell you. Is it her grey eyes whose look penetrates you like a gimlet, and remains fixed in you like the head of an arrow? It is rather, I think, her gentle, seducing smile, which remains on her face like a mask. Her gentle grace penetrates you by degrees, emanates from her like a perfume from her slim figure, which scarcely sways as she passes you, for she seems to glide rather than to walk, from her pretty somewhat drawling voice, which seems to be the music of her smile, from her gestures also, which are never violent, and which intoxicate the eyes by their harmoniousness. For three years I saw only her on earth! How I suffered! For she deceived me with everybody! Why? For no reason except that she wanted to deceive me. And when I found out and when I treated her like a low strumpet; she said calmly, 'Pray, are we married?'"

"Since I have been here, I have thought about her so much, that I have begun to understand her. She is Manon Lescaut over again. That Manon who could not love without deceiving, Manon to whom love, pleasure and money signify one and the same thing."

He stopped for a few minutes, and then continued: "When I had spent my last halfpenny on her, she said to me quite simply: 'You understand my dear fellow, that I cannot live on air and time. I am very fond of you, I like you better than I do anyone else, but I must live. Poverty and I should never agree well together.'

"And yet, if I were to tell you what a terrible life I led with her! When I looked at her I felt as much inclined to kill her as to kiss her. When I looked at her I felt a furious longing to open my arms, to clasp her in them and to strangle her. In her, behind her eyes, there was something treacherous and indefinable which made me hate her, and that is, perhaps, the reason why I love her so much. In her the Feminine, the hateful and maddening Feminine, was more powerful than in any other woman. She was charged with it, surcharged with it, like with an intoxicating and venomous fluid. She was a Woman, more than any other ever was.

"And then, when I used to go out with her, she looked at the men in such a manner, that she seemed to give herself to each of them, by a mere glance, and that exasperated me, and yet attached me to her all the more. That creature belonged to everyone as she went through the streets, in spite of me, in spite of herself, by her very nature, although she looked so modest and gentle. Do you understand me?

"And what torture! In the theatre and when we went to a restaurant, it seemed to me as if men were embracing her under my very eyes. And as soon as I left her alone, the others came up to her, as a matter of fact, and now I have not seen her for ten years, and I love her more than ever!"

It was quite dark by this time and the strong scent from the orange trees floated through the air.

"Shall you see her again?" I asked him.

"By Jove! In land and money I have now from seven to eight hundred thousand francs, and when I have accumulated a million, I shall sell everything and return to Paris. I shall have enough for one year with her—one delicious year. And then, goodbye, my life will be closed."

"And what afterwards?" I said.

"Afterwards, I do not know. It will be finished! Perhaps I shall ask her to engage me as her footman."

THE HARVEST HOME

THE sickle was heard on all sides, whilst songs, now merry as the lark's, now passionate as the nightingale's, rose from the fields, for harvest was in full swing. The wide plain was waving in the light summer breeze, like a yellow sea, here and there great waves seemed to rise and fall, whilst spots were full of reapers, who looked like small black insects.

Till that day I had been the prisoner of Russian hospitality, in the house of a nobleman of Eastern Gallicia. It was a long building, situated on a hill, and stood level with the ground, with stables, sheds, coach-houses and barns attached. A footpath wound through the fields to the village, past a flat, bare, mound of earth, which the peasants called the Tartars' Hill, and on the other side of it was a cornfield, from which the reapers' songs proceeded.

I took my gun and went out of the house, and saw my host, Wasyl Lesnowicy, sitting under the verandah. He was a venerable-looking, tall, bony man, with a high forehead, thick, white hair, a long beard, a Roman nose and broad chin, and his blue eyes, beneath his thick eyebrows, were bright and piercing.

"Do not go too far from the house, old friend," he said. "The harvest will be all over this evening, and we shall celebrate our *Harvest Home* tonight, and the whole village will come. They feel an attachment for us, because we belong to them, but over there, amongst our Polish neighbours, nobody goes to the *Harvest Home*, except the paid reapers."

Herr Wasyl was proud of the esteem in which he was held amongst the country people. His family, like all the families in Eastern Gallicia, of Russian descent, had adopted the Polish language and sentiments under Polish rule, but had adhered to the Greek Church. He had never treated his peasants harshly, but, prior to 1848, he had looked upon this restoration of the Polish monarchy, as a political necessity. When the serfs were emancipated in that year, and Russian nationality awoke to new life in Gallicia, Wasyl began to take in Russian newspapers, to buy Russian books, to have his daughters' dressed in Russian fashions, to speak French with the Poles, and when he spoke with the peasants, to use such phrases as: "we brothers, we fellow countrymen."

I told him I was only going to the reapers, wished him good-morning, and went towards the village, and in the path through the fields I met a slim peasant woman, with a bright coloured handkerchief wound round her head, like a turban, who wished me "good-morning" as she passed me with downcast eyes.

I got to the field of corn, which was falling rapidly beneath the strong arms of the reapers. The young fellows were working vigorously, in their coarse linen trousers and shirts, with their feet, arms and sunburnt-necks bare, and wearing broad-brimmed, straw hats, and the girls, in short, bright-coloured dresses and flapping chemises and with red or yellow handkerchiefs on their heads, rose up and down like large poppies as they reaped.

By the side of the path there stood a great jug of water, with a loaf of black bread as a cover, whilst some peasants were setting up sheaves with real Russian gravity, and stacking them in a slanting direction, like soldiers stack arms, so that the rain might run off them.

Some boys were hiding amongst them, and one called out, "I am a bear! This is my cave!" whilst the others tried to drive him out. A reaper, a young woman, was standing on one side, whose dusty feet, slender hips and full bosom were particularly well-shaped.

Her hair was wound in a great coil round her small head with its animated blue eyes, and delicate, slightly curved nose. She wiped the perspiration from her face with the wide sleeve of her chemise, put the sickle into the band of her apron behind, and sat down amongst the corn, where her child was lying. She took it to her bosom, sat down under the whitethorn, where there was shade, and spoke to it with words that were as sweet as kisses, with tender diminutives such as no other language possesses, half singing, half twittering, so that a robin grew attentive, flew towards hers, and watched her closely with a pair of very intelligent black eyes, from the topmost branch.

They all greeted me, and then scanned me attentively, and just then an old peasant came along the path.

The next field belonged to him, and he was super-intending his people at work, and, having seen me, came with the innate politeness of our Russian peasants, to keep me company. Ten yards off, he took off his hat, and wished my grandchildren and my great grandchildren unmeasured prosperity.

He had a somewhat melancholy face, with a white moustache and grey hair, and wore a grey coat of coarse, shaggy cloth, with a hood, and blue braid on the seams, a coat such as Ghengis Kahn's horse-men may have worn, and which the Gallician peasant adheres to in his dress, as a heritage from the Tartar period.

We walked up and down amongst the sheaves, spoke of the harvest, and gradually got up to the Tartars' Hill, which stood out like a black coffin against the setting sun, so I rested my gun against it, and sat down in the shade. The peasant thought for a moment, looked about him, and then also sat down, some little distance off.

The less I spoke, the more the old man tried to entertain me.

"We shall finish today," he said, "and the people from the mansion also, and then we shall keep our harvest home together."

"So you are on friendly terms with your former landlord?"

"Why not?" the peasant replied. "He is one of us, he is a Russian like us.

"It is different with the Polish landlords, and is an old standing feud; our popular ballads mention it, but Zur Lesnowiczy behaves to us, so to speak, as a brother to his brothers. He helped us to build the school, and gave a wood, about which there was a dispute, up to us, so we shall elect him as our Deputy,"

"You have a good school here, and, from what I can see, agriculture is in a better state here than in other parts of Gallicia."

"It is in a tolerably fair state here," the farmer said, quickly; "but can one be surprised that it is in a worse state in other places? You can read in many books, that the peasants here are lazy, bad workers, and regular drunkards and block-heads; the choir-master told us this once, but that is not true now, thank God, though nobody could be surprised if it were.

"You must remember how it used to be with us. When Poland was a kingdom, we were good for nothing, except to work on the noblemens' land, just like horses or oxen; only, if his neighbour lost one of his horses, he had to pay him an indemnity, but if he killed one of his peasants, he often had to pay nothing. How could the peasant possibly care for the land, and cultivate it carefully, when he was treated like a stranger or like a brute.

"Then we were incorporated into the Austrian Empire, and matters immediately became better. The peasant was then a man like any other man, but the land remained the property of the nobleman; and the peasant was obliged to do him compulsory service.

"'The great Emperor Joseph,' and the peasant took off his hat and put it on again, "gave us a charter which stated clearly the peasant was to work so many days for the lord of the manor, and so many days for himself, and that was fair for both parties. But the nobility did not wish for justice, and managed to evade the charter. I will tell you how, immediately.

"We love our children, and it is hard for a father to part with his son. Now, let us suppose that a peasant had thirty acres of land, on which he could live comfortably, and had to give four days compulsory labour for it. Then the nobleman, the lord of the manor, would come and say:

"'You have two strong sons, who will have to go for soldiers, but you do not wish to part me with them. Do you know what you must do? Give both of them ten acres, then each of you will have ten, and each of you will give me four days compulsory service.' Their sons divided the land amongst themselves again, and the grandsons again, and the compulsory service increased, and if a peasant at any time united all these portions of land, he often had to give twenty-four days compulsory service in the month, instead of four, and asked himself how he was to manage it."

"But I think that formerly the peasants were not as averse from labour as they are now," I said after a time; "for in those days, after working all day for the lord of the manor, they used to work for themselves at night in the moonlight.

"That was so, and the peasant took to drinking in order to forget his misery. Spirits made him oblivious for a time, and that was a good thing. They sang, they danced, they talked about this and that, and different persons; they pawned their coats and boots, but still they managed to live. In 1848, however, everything was suddenly altered. We are free, the land belongs to us, and our former landlord is nothing more now than a neighbour, and since then, everything has improved. The peasant attends carefully to his land, and makes money by it; it is good land about here, there could scarcely be better soil, and farming is a pleasure.

"Years ago, I was punished sometimes for neglecting my compulsory labour, and half my land used to lie in waste; now I rent a farm from a Polish landlord, and it is worth looking at. Just look at Sieniawa; every house in the village is built of stone, and the roads are good. That is, of course, only a beginning, for the taxes still weigh heavily on us, and in most places we still want railways, good roads and schools."

I looked at the peasant in surprise.

"But I have been told that you are not particularly fond of schools," I said.

The old man folded his arms on his chest, and swayed himself backwards and forwards.

"What nonsense people talk! That was only the case whilst everything was still Polish, and we did not like to pay for our children to unlearn their mother tongue, but now our children are taught in Russian, and the villages are building schools themselves, and paying all that is necessary."

Meanwhile a number of women and young fellows had surrounded the whitethorn, and suddenly they began to shout and scream. The old farmer sat up and looked about him, and just then, a half-grown boy, with bare feet, and long, tangled yellow hair came running to the Tartars' mound, and shouted, half out of breath, and from a distance:

"Grandfather! Grandfather! . . . the old . . . women will not give . . . Jewa the harvest wreath."

"Why not?" the farmer asked.

"They say her morals are bad!"

"What has that to do with the old women? But they are like hens, they peck any young one that comes amongst them. Just look at that boy; how the cockerel already knows how to defend his pullet! Come with me, sir, you shall decide who is to have the harvest wreath. There are some very pretty girls amongst them, so that the choice is difficult."

We went down the hill, past the waggons that were being loaded, and the reapers, who were sharpening their sickles, and under the whitethorn we saw five young women making the harvest wreath. Two of them had their laps full of ears of yellow corn, the third had blue cornflowers in her apron, and from time to time put one into the wreath, and one was holding a scented pink ribbon in her brown hands, and was singing.

One, however, was sitting apart from the others, with her head resting in both her hands, as if absorbed in thought, and her eyelashes reminded me of black shadows. A number of women, children, and young fellows were squabbling, shouting and laughing round her, but she did not look up. We went up to them, and they were silent, but she did not raise her eyes, and the old peasant bent over her with his hands resting on his knees.

"Well, Jewa, won't they give you the wreath?" she looked up for a moment, and I saw a face whose outlines were as lovely as those of a Phebe of Greek sculpture, but pale, very pale, with two flaming eyes, and her uncovered bosom rose and fell slowly, like a sleeping swan moves its wings. Her eyelashes drooped again, and she looked at the wreath apathetically.

I looked at her again, and said eagerly:

"The wreath belongs to her."

The old farmer nodded, whilst the reapers ran up, waving their hats and crying:

"Jewa is to wear the wreath!"

She got up, and looked at me, but she hardly appeared grateful; then, with a proud movement of her head, she threw the long, thick plaits over her shoulders in front, and began to undo one of them.

"Choose the girls who are to crown me," she said, smiling disdainfully, to the reapers who were looking at her, and then, turning her back on them, she rapidly undid her plaits, and spread her long, soft hair around her like a cloak.

Nobody said a word, only an old toothless woman came close to me and said in a whisper: "It is easy for that idle thing to have a white complexion and long hair, for she does nothing but dream, love and laugh."

"Where is Handza?" a young reaper asked shyly, with his eyes on the ground.

"Come along! Come along!" the old peasant said, pulling the peasant girl by the sleeve of her chemise, who, however, resisted awkwardly, and threw her red apron over her blushing face.

"You know that you deserve it, if there is any justice on earth," the old woman continued. "Do you not like her?"

All right," many of them cried. "She will do. Choose the other."

Half-a-dozen female names were heard at the same time, but *Basja* resounded most frequently. *Basja! Basja!* The old man raised his hand,

"All right," he cried, "the majority say *Basja*, is she to be the other?"

The reapers agreed, and *Basja*, who was a little fat thing, carried her head, with its snub nose, and flashing eyes rather high.

"Get ready," the old woman said. "The sun has set." The two girls took the wreath, raised it over Jewa's head, and placed it gently on it. She immediately took it in both hands and set it straight, and then stood before us with folded arms, her golden crown of corn on her loose, waving hair, looking at us indifferently, as the *harvest queen*.

The other two girls also decorated themselves with flowers; crowds of reapers had come from different directions, peasants from the village, and at last the musicians. They began to tune their instruments, the people jostled each other with shouts and laughter, and the old farmer arranged the procession, whilst other landed proprietors stood about and discussed the elections which were soon coming on.

At last we set off; the musicians first, a smart young fellow, in a black cap made of lambs' skin, with a fiddle, backed up by a fat farmer in black cloth coat and trousers, who was playing another, the village shepherd, who was playing the flute, whilst a dark-complexioned fellow in his shirt sleeves and linen trousers, banged the cymbals, and the little choir-master played the violoncello with great dignity.

After them, came the Harvest queen, haughty in her pride of beauty and victory, accompanied by the two other girls; then came the peasant and the reapers, one in a linen jacket and trousers, another with a shaggy cloth coat over his shoulders, in straw hats, barefooted, or in heavy boots, the women with bright red shawls wound round their heads like turbans, the girls with long plaits and great yellow mallows stuck in their hair, and wearing coral necklaces, and all merry.

The musicians struck up, and from more than a hundred voices there rose up the old, heathen Bacchanalian, solemn, melancholy harvest song, and the waggon, drawn by four small horses followed slowly in the ruts through the field, whilst all who had remained behind now joined the procession as it went through the village.

Outside the wooden moss-grown church, there stood a huge, grey stone, with curious, half obliterated characters on it. The reapers halted there, and Jewa came slowly forward, took off her wreath and laid it on the stone, whilst the priest came out of the church in his surplice, with the holy water sprinkler, and blessed the wreath and reapers and it was strange to see Jewa stand by the stone with her glittering, black hair, take the wreath of corn and put it on her head again, whilst all the people were on their knees round her.

Close to the church was the judge's house, and as the reapers went by, he was standing at his door with a cock under his arm. He tied its feet, and then fastened it to the harvest wreath on Jewa's hood.

They all looked at the bird; as soon as the judge let it go, it tried to fly, clapped its wings and crowed, which was the sign of a good harvest next year.

The reapers cheered, the musicians played, and the judge and his wife walked about with a bottle of brandy in their hand, and drank with everybody. Then they joined the procession and started for the Manor House.

The harvest song sounded over the plain, the fiddles squeaked, the reapers shouted a Russian *Evoe*, the cock went on crowing, and over the little wood, the red disc of the moon was rising.

Mr. Wasyl Lesnowiczy was standing rubbing his hands outside his house, and by his side stood his wife, Athanasia, Xenia Lesnowiczowa, in a check dress, and with a pink cap on her clay-coloured hair, whilst her fat-faced, snub-nosed son stood by her side, with his pretty little wife on his arm.

The reapers formed a semi-circle round her, and when everybody was silent, Jewa gave them their congratulations.

"We have brought you the harvest wreath, may God bless you and yours, give us a prosperous year, and a good harvest!"

"Many years! Many years!" the reapers exclaimed, and Mr. Lesnowiczy thanked them for himself and his.

Jewa took the wreath from her head, the cock crowed again, and then she gave the symbol to the mistress of the house, who put a coral necklace round her throat, whilst the younger women gave small presents to the two other girls. The servants brought out

rough, deal tables, covered them with bottles of brandy, great cheeses, Russian sausages, which looked like
gigantic, young snakes, loaves of bread, and dishes of
pork, of which they were heartily invited to partake.

The younger gentlemen gave the harvest queen one
arm, whilst he offered the other to her two attendants,
old Lesnowiczy dragged a resisting brother peasant
and elector to the table, the choir-master called out
continually:

"Make yourselves at home, good people!" at the
same time gnawing a huge sausage, the other end of
which was on the ground, whilst he clutched a brandy
bottle in the other hand.

The staid landowners remained at table once they
had sat down, and drank glass after glass of brandy,
but the young people hardly waited to snatch a mor-
sel, before they got ready to dance. Mr. Lesnowiczy
twirled round with the harvest queen, let her go, and
for a few moments turned heavily round by himself,
like a bumble-bee that has fallen into a glass, and a
young fellow stepped out of the ranks of the reapers,
threw his oily hair back, wiped his mouth with his
shirt sleeve, and offered the younger lady his arm.

Soon they were all stamping about in the wildest
excitement, the precentor took a bite at his sausage
from time to time, and then scraped away viciously
at his violoncello, which groaned beneath his vigorous bow, the cymbal seemed to be weeping, and the
fiddles screamed, at one time like naughty children,
at another like dying people calling for help, half mad
with terror.

They grew merry at table. One handed his glass to the other; it shook and spilt, and the other took it in the same manner, but it was all done ceremoniously, and with polite speeches.

"May your worthy wife remain healthy for many years, may God bless her, and grant you peace, and that you may always come to a good understanding together."

"So be it."

Then the other bent his head to the right and left:

"Many years, so be it," he replied; "God grant it and to you, also, tenfold, brother."

Then they kissed one another on the right cheek, and then on the other, and the second man emptied the glass; the conversation was general and noisy, but, in spite of the differences of opinion, there was no quarrelling or disputing, and yet our peasants are more obstinate in their opinions than the most obstinate Germans.

There was a movement amongst the dancers, and a young man came in, who was a peasant, by his dress, but from his gun, he looked like a gamekeeper. His upright bearing struck those who saw him, but his glance did so still more.

"That is Dmito," our host said, in reply to my question; "he is under game-keeper, and a strange fellow, but as honest and faithful as a hound. He shall dance the kolomijka for us."

Mr. Lesnowiczy went up to him, and the young woman said:

"He plays an important part in this neighbourhood. All the women run after him, but he has a sensible head on his shoulders. Jewa has bewitched him, as you will see by-and-bye."

The musicians struck up the kolomijka, and the dancers, with their arms round each others' waists, quickly formed a circle, in which stood Jewa and the game-keeper.

The first sounds rose into the air singly, with a melancholy cadence; the game-keeper stood motionless, with his arms crossed on his breast, and his head bent, as if in pain. He accompanied the music in a low voice by a sad song, but from time to time, a sound, a sigh, loud weeping, a cry of distress rose melodiously from his breast, whilst at a good distance from him, Jewa stood quietly, with her eyes fixed steadfastly on him, and her head raised proudly, as if she were altogether out of his reach.

The music rose passionately to a wonderful melody, and suddenly he threw up his head, uttered a cry, a wild huntsman's shout, the scream of an eagle that is darting on its prey. Then he raised his arms and began to dance, now like a child at play, now like a juggler taming a serpent, now like a beast of prey following his mate in wild bounds. He never took his eyes off hers, every step, every motion of his body was intended for her; she, however, watched him coolly and avoided him, and the magic circles which he drew round her nearer and nearer, until he was close to her, and the music grew wilder and wilder, until he was by her side with a leap, and threw his arm round her neck like a hook.

But at the same instant, she escaped from him at a bound, and danced insolently and mockingly at the other end of the ring of spectators, who laughed loudly, with her hands on her hips, as if to challenge him again.

Again the dancer stood motionless, with drooping head, again he approached Jewa, and again she escaped him, until at last he seemed to be in despair, his dancing became the apathetic movements of an unhappy lover, and his song suddenly turned to weeping; but she mocked him with joyous trills, she threw her head back, laughed, and made fun of him, and danced round him like a moth round a candle. He, however, fell to the ground as if he were dying, but jumped up the next moment, threw his arms like a noose round Jewa's waist, and she was his.

Then, amidst the frenzied applause of the spectators they danced together, the fiddle and cymbals exulted, the dance became a wedding dance, and their song a wedding hymn.

Meanwhile, the landowners at the table were singing the refrain of a jovial drinking song, which Nikolaus Lesnowiczy had started. The old gentleman was rather too merry, kissed his wife before their guests, and called her a confounded flirt, whilst she blinked her eyes in confusion, and I went slowly across the yard, where the fowls were asleep, and the dog growled, but began to wag his tail, when he saw who it was.

There was not a sound to be heard behind the house, and I went into a small meadow and lay down on a cock of hay. Everything was perfectly silent all round, no cry of a bird, no sound of a shepherd's pipe, a damp mist was rising, the extensive plain was flooded in moonlight, and the sky was covered with stars, and the Milky Way was bright and clear. Suddenly, I heard a nightingale quite near, most likely in a clump of trees close to me, that were illuminated by the moon. Another replied, and the sweet sounds were carried far in the perfect stillness of the night. The short, dry grass crackled and broke, and I heard stealthy footsteps, and the tender, alluring cry of a cat in a meadow. The footsteps came nearer and nearer, and I sat up; it was a woman, who suddenly stopped, as if in alarm; it was Jewa.

"Is that you, sir?" she said, calmly.

I took her hand. "Whom are you looking for?" I asked, but she gave me no answer, though she bore my gaze without flinching. "You are looking for the game-keeper," I continued." She did not reply, nor look down, but her eyes blazed, and pupils grew as large as those of a cat wandering about in the moonlight.

"You are not looking for him?"

"Yes, I am," she replied, in a low but decided voice. "You can but call me names for doing it."

"Why should I call you names?" I asked.

"Because everybody does; because it is the way of the world," she replied, firmly, looking me straight in the face.

"I am not calling you any names."

"Then you also make fun of this world of ours," she replied, with a contemptuous laugh, which was carried far away in the silence until it was lost in the distance. The nightingale ceased, and even the cat was quiet.

"What do I care for people, what is the opinion of the world to me? Just as much as a poor robber from the Carpathian mountains cares for the gallows."

I released her hand, and she drew her chemise together over her half-naked, classical bust.

"None of them are as beautiful as I am. The priest looks at me reprovingly at certain passages in his sermons, but if he meets me alone in the forest, he slaps me on the neck or thighs with his fat hand. They call me names, because I cannot be a hypocrite, like them, and their wives and daughters. Because I look at a man, if he pleases me, because I talk with him, if he amuses me, because I . . ."

"Well?"

"Because I kiss him, if I love him, and because, if he is sick with love for me I say to him: 'Come to me tonight!' Do we live only in order that we may have an honoured grave——"

"Then get married."

"I will not," she replied, proudly; "I will never sell myself to any man, as if I were a head of cattle, and belong to him whenever he pleases. I will be free, and remain a wild cat amongst the tame ones. I laugh at this world."

Again the dry grass crackled. Jewa listened, and, for a moment, she stood motionless, in the moonlight with her arm raised; then she ran away, and I returned to the mansion and went under the verandah, where, leaning against the wooden balcony, I looked down into the throng of the harvest home. Nobody was intoxicated, but all were merry. The Cossack was laying about him furiously, with bandaged eyes, with his back to the pot, and kicking, so that each time it seemed as if he were going to kick it to pieces. They had made a fire at the foot of the mound, and were dancing round it wildly; old Stephen was standing amongst the tables' and singing a Cossack song in a cracked voice, which the choirmaster accompanied on the violoncello, shaking his head all the time.

Then Mr. Nikola, with half-drunken looks, beckoned to two young men, and the three went softly out of the house together, and I looked after them. The merry fellows cowered down in a thicket, and suddenly began a mocking song. The refrain especially was very like the melody of cats, but the girl for whom it was intended, was sitting on a bough of the willow tree, and Dimitro, the game-keeper, was at her feet, with his handsome head resting on her lap, and she buried both her hands almost wildly in his curls, and laughed.

THE NEW WIFE

THERE was a large fire burning in the grate, and on a Japanese table there were two tea cups, whilst the tea pot was smoking by the side of the sugar basin, which was flanked by a decanter of rum.

Count de Sallure threw his hat, his gloves and fur-lined overcoat into a chair, whilst the Countess, having got rid of her wraps, was arranging her hair in front of the looking-glass. She smiled at herself, with an air of satisfaction, whilst she arranged the little curls on her temples with her delicate fingers, which glistened with rings. Then she turned to her husband, who had been looking at her for some moments, and seemed to be hesitating, as if some private thought were troubling him, and at last he said:

"Did you have enough attention paid you this evening."

She looked him in the face, with her eyes full of triumph and defiance, and then she replied:

"I should hope so."

She sat down in her chair, and he, taking a place opposite to her, went on, as he broke a piece of cake:

"It was almost ridiculous . . . for me!"

"Do you mean to make a scene?" she asked. "Do you intend what you have said as a reproach?"

"No, my dear, I am only saying that the way in which Monsieur Burel went on with you was almost unbecoming. If . . . if . . . if I had a right to do so, I should have got angry."

"Pray be candid; you do not think at present, like you did a year ago, that is all. When I found out that you had a mistress, a mistress whom you loved, I saw also that you did not care whether anyone paid me attentions or not. I told you my trouble, I said to you, just as you said to someone this evening, only with more reason: 'You are compromising Madame de Sevry, you are causing me pain, and are making yourself ridiculous? And what was your reply? Oh! you let me clearly understand that I was free, that amongst sensible people, marriage was nothing but an association of their common interests, a social, but not a moral tie. Is not that true? You gave me to understand that your mistress was much more preferable than me, more seductive, more of a woman! That was what you said: 'More of a woman.' It was naturally all veiled with that consideration which a well-bred man always shows, wrapped up in compliments, said with a delicacy to which I render full justice. But I understood it perfectly, nevertheless.

"We then agreed to live together for the future, but completely separated, had a child, which formed a bond of union between us. You, however, almost gave me to understand that you only cared for appearances, that if I liked I could take a lover, provided the matter were kept a secret. You spoke at length, and very well on woman's ingenuity, and their cleverness in saving appearances, etc., etc."

"I understood you, my dear, I understood you perfectly. At that time you were very much in love with Madame de Sevry, and my legitimate, my legal affection was in your way, and no doubt I deprived you of some of your resources, and so since then we have lived apart. We go into society together, and receive company together, and then we each of us, go to our own room; now, however, for the last month or two, you have assumed the ways of a jealous man. What is the meaning of it?"

"My dear, I am not jealous, but I am afraid of seeing you compromise yourself. You are young, lively, adventurous . . ."

"I beg your pardon, if we speak of adventures, I must beg you to strike the balance between us."

"Come, do not joke, please. I am speaking to you seriously, as a friend. As to everything that you have been saying, it is very much exaggerated."

"Not at all. You acknowledged your intrigue, which is equivalent to authorizing me to imitate you. I have not done so."

"Allow me . . ."

"Please let me speak, I did not do so; I have no lover, and I have not had one . . . up to the present. I am waiting . . . I am on the look out but I cannot find one. I want someone nice . . . nicer than you . . . I am paying you a compliment, and you do not seem to see it."

"My dear, all these jokes are absolutely out of place."

"I am not joking in the least. You have spoken to me about the eighteenth century, and given me to understand that you believe in the days of the regency, I have not forgotten it, and on the day when it suits me to cease to be what I am, it will be no good for you to try and prevent it, you will be, without even suspecting it . . . a cuckold like the rest."

"Oh! How can you use such words?"

"Such words! . . .Why you laughed like a madman when Madame de Gers declared that Monsieur de Servy looked like a cuckold who was hunting for his horns."

"What may sound funny from Madame de Gers' lips, becomes unbecoming in yours."

"Not at all! But you think that word cuckold very funny when it is applied to Monsieur de Sevry, and that it has a very unpleasant sound, when applied to you. It all depends upon how you look at it; but I do not care about the word particularly; I only used it to see whether you were ripe."

"Ripe . . . ripe for what?"

"For becoming one. If a man grow angry when he hears that word, it is a sign that . . . he is near it. In two months you will laugh if I speak of a man . . . who wears the horns. Yes . . . of course . . . when a man is one, he does not notice it."

"You are particularly rude this evening. I never saw you like it before."

"Oh! So I have changed for the worse now . . . It is altogether your fault."

"Come my dear, let us talk seriously. I beg and entreat you not to allow Monsieur Burel's unbecoming attentions, like you did this evening."

"So you are jealous! I said so."

"No, no, I only do not wish to be ridiculous. And if I see this gentleman speaking to you again, on to your shoulders, or rather on to your bosom . . ."

"He was looking for a speaking-trumpet."

"I . . . I shall pull his ears,"

"Do you happen to be in love with me?"

"One might easily be with a less pretty woman."

"Oh! So that is what you feel! But I am not in love with you, anymore!"

The count got up, and going round the small table, he went behind his wife and pressed a kiss on the nape of her neck, but she shook him off, and looking at him fixedly, she said:

"None of such pleasantries between you and me, if you please. We live apart; it is all over."

"Come, do not be angry. I have thought you charming for some time."

"Well . . . then . . . I have been the gainer. You also . . . think me . . . ripe!"

"I think that you are delightful, my dear; you have arms, a complexion, shoulders . . ."

"Which would delight Monsieur Burel."

"You are cruel but there . . . really . . . I do not know any woman who is so attractive as you are."

"You are fasting."

"Eh?"

"I say, you are fasting."

"What do you mean?"

"When one is fasting, one is hungry, and when one is hungry, one makes up one's mind to eat things which one would not care for at another time. I am

the dish . . . which you have neglected for a long time,
but which you would not mind tasting . . . tonight."

"Oh! Marguerite! Who has taught you to talk like
that?"

"You! Look here: Since your rupture with Madame
de Sevry, you have had, to my knowledge, four mistresses, dressmakers and actresses amongst them. Then
how can I explain your . . . inclinations this evening,
but by a momentary fast?"

"I will be frank and brutal, without any attempts
at politeness. I have grown amorous of you again;
really, very amorous. There."

"So! So! Then you would like to make things-up?"

"Yes, I should."

"Tonight?"

"Oh! Marguerite!"

"All right, there you are scandalized again. Let us
understand one another, my dear. We are nothing to
each other now, is that not so? I am your wife, it is
true, but your wife—who has her full liberty. I was
going to accept an engagement elsewhere, and you
ask me to let you have the preference. I will give it
you . . . for the same price."

"I do not understand you."

"I will explain myself. Am I as nice as your dressmakers and actresses? Be open."

"A thousand times nicer."

"Well, how much did the nicest of them cost you
in three months?"

"I cannot remember."

"I ask you: How much did the most charming of
your mistresses cost you in three months in money,

jewels, dinners, suppers, the theatre etc., the whole thing in fact?"

"How can I tell?"

"You ought to know. Come, a moderate price. Five thousand francs a month will be about it?"

"Yes . . . about."

"Very well my dear friend, give me five thousand francs every month, and I will belong to you for a month, from this evening."

"You must be mad!"

"If you take it like that, I will wish you goodnight."

The countess rose and went into her bedroom. The bed was turned back, and a vague perfume impregnated the hangings, and the count appeared in the door, and observed:

"How nice it smells here."

"Really? . . . It is the same as ever; nothing has been altered."

"Very strange . . . It smells very nice."

"Possibly. But will you kindly leave the room, because I want to go to bed."

"Marguerite!"

"Please leave the room!"

His reply was to come quite in, and to take an easy chair, and the countess continued:

"Oh! So that is it! Very well then, so much the worse for you."

She took off her ball dress very slowly, and then raised her bare, white arms over her head, to take her hair down in front of the looking-glass and something pink appeared at the top of her black silk stays, beneath a cloud of lace; the count rose hastily and came towards her, but she said:

162

"Don't come near me, or I shall get angry."

By way of an answer, however, he took her into his arms and sought her lips, but she stopped suddenly, seized a glass of perfumed water for her teeth, which was standing on her toilette table, and threw it over her shoulders, right into her husband's face, who got up furious, dripping with water, and said:

"That was very stupid."

"It may be . . . But you know my conditions: Five thousand francs."

"Why, I should be an idiot! . . ."

"Why so?"

"What do you mean by 'Why so'? A husband to pay for sleeping in the room as his wife! . . ."

"Oh! what horrid words you use! . . ."

"That is possible, but I repeat, that a man would be an idiot to pay his wife, his lawful wife."

"It is far more idiotic to pay actresses and those sort of women, when one has a lawful wife."

"That may be, but I do not want to be ridiculous."

The countess sat down on the couch, and slowly took off one of her stockings, pulling it inside out and her little rosy leg came out of its mauve satin covering and her little foot rested on the carpet.

The count came a little nearer, and in a tender voice he said:

"What a funny idea that is of yours!"

"What idea?"

"To ask five thousand francs."

"Nothing more natural. We are strangers to one another, are we not? Well, you want me, and you cannot marry me, because we are married already, and so you buy me, and give rather less for me, perhaps, than you would for another woman. Just think then. This money, instead of going to a horrid woman, who would do I do not know what with it, will remain in your house, and be partly devoted to your household expenses. And then, what can there be more amusing and more original for a clever man, than to pay his own wife? In illicit love affairs, men only care for what costs a great deal. You will set a new value on our . . . legitimate love, and will impart to it a flavour of debauchery, a spice of . . . nastiness by putting a tariff on it, like love for which you have to pay. Is that not so?"

She got up almost naked, and went to her dressing-room, and said:

"Now, Monsieur, please go, or I shall ring for my maid."

But the count, who had also risen, and was standing in the middle of the room, perplexed and put out, suddenly threw a pocket-book at her and said:

"There are six thousand, you baggage . . . But you know . . ."

The countess picked up the money, counted it and said in a low voice:

"What?"

"Do not make a habit of it."

She, however, began to laugh, and going up to him, she said:

"Five thousand francs every month, Monsieur, or I shall send you back to your actresses. And perhaps if . . . if you are very well satisfied I shall ask for an increase."

AN AMERICAN DUEL

BARONESS AMELIA was one of those ladies in the fashionable world, who after having been brought up very strictly and Jesuitically in a convent, was married to a wealthy man who was her equal in rank, but who was quite unintellectual, and whom she did not love. She very soon began to enjoy and love, which she had hitherto only seen from a distance, to the full, and tried to avenge herself on her husband and her parents for the unhappy years of her girlhood, and the threatened monotony of her married life, which by a dissoluteness of life which reminded those who knew her, of some Russian Empress of the last century. Nature, which had lavishly bestowed upon her every gift which might make a man happy, at the same time had given her that charm she required in her frivolous mode of life, in order not only to keep the unfortunate men who were taken in her toils, as long as her caprice lasted, but also to spurn them from her insolently with her little foot whenever she pleased, and to tyrannize over them from a distance, and so to prevent any scandal. Baroness Amelia was of middle height, neither too thin nor too voluptuously full, but she possessed that perfect symmetry of shape, which we admire so much in the Greek statues of Venus, and with all her alluring and dominating womanhood, the expression of her regular features, had something charmingly girl-like like in it. She knew how to walk to perfection, how to throw herself on a couch and lie back in an easy chair. She could talk well, and was at the same time a handsome woman, and a high bred, aristocratic lady.

She had just got rid of a young member of the aristocracy, who had compromised her by his devoted attentions, and the time was always hanging very heavily on her hands, when she met a young, very good-looking man in the street, whose looks and manner had something original and even strange about them. A lady with whom she happened to be, told her he was a young artist, and said that his name was Maximilian A———.

"I must have him," the young Messalina said to herself, and immediately the pursuit began. As open as she met him, she gave him an ardent, provocative look from her dark, bright eyes; if she was in a box at the theatre and saw his light, curly head in the pit she kept her opera glasses fixed on him during the whole performance. Maximilian saw all this perfectly, and as an intrigue with a handsome member of the aristocracy took his fancy very much, he began to walk up and down in front of her windows and once, when he met her by herself, he immediately followed her. She turned off into a small side street, where there was very little traffic, and he understood the hint, followed her and acquaintance was made. She soon found a pretext for asking him to her house, and before a week was over, she belonged to him, or rather, he belonged to her. Maximilian, who had at first been drawn to the highly born, charming woman, merely from vanity, got more and more deeply involved in the toils of her coquetry, which she laid so skilfully, and at last he loved her with all the ardour of his eccentric, artistic nature. The lady, who had hitherto only carried on love intrigues, but who had never been really loved, took great pleasure in his enthusiastic adoration, and in time she became really and deeply attached to the young artist.

Then, however, something happened which suddenly dragged the proud beauty from her heaven. Maximilian was young, handsome and fashionable, and had those high-bred manners which so easily become dangerous to women, but, like so many other artists, he had the misfortune to be of a morbidly nervous temperament, and this made him vacillating and even cowardly.

One summer, when the Baroness was staying at her villa at Baden near Vienna, she made an appointment with him on the Calvarienberg, and lost herself with him in the neighbouring wood, and amidst their love making and joking, they did not notice how late it was, and so night overtook them on the way home. They wandered about, missed their road, and got further and further into the wood, and when the trees looked as if they were alive, when strange figures stretched their long undefined arms, and the owls began to hoot, she suddenly felt that the man to whom she had trusted herself was trembling as she held his arm.

What a discovery for a living woman! For a woman can overlook everything in a man, ugliness, vulgarity, coarseness, stupidity, anything except cowardice.

From that time, the Baroness merely endured him near her, as she had lost all love for him, and consequently she longed for another man, and fate willed it that a man appeared on the scenes just at the right time who was the exact opposite to Maximilian. His name was Stefan K——, a Hungarian and a Colonel of Hussars. He was not very tall, but well made, nearly forty and of great manly beauty. His face, which was as brown as a gypsy's, had a winning, almost tender look, but his large dark eyes sparkled with courage, and even a sort of wildness, which impressed men, and made women rave about him. Baroness Amelia also fell in love with him the first time she saw him, and he, who was in the habit of making easy conquests, took her by storm. Then they rode together, shot at a small target with saloon pistols and the artistic lady, suddenly became an enthusiastic Amazon. Once, when the colonel had just loaded the pistols again, the baroness said:

"Today we will shoot at cards."

"With pleasure," he replied, "but I know beforehand that you will put me to shame, for your hand and eye are more sure than mine, and you shoot better."

"Oh! I learnt to shoot from my brothers when I was quite a little girl, so that accounts for it," she said.

The colonel fastened the four aces to a wooden pole, against which the target usually hung, and she cut out the club, the diamond, the heart, the spade, one after the other. The colonel was delighted, and called out *bravo*, and the Baroness said:

"Do you know what I should like you to do but I do not suppose you will risk it?"

"There is nothing in the world for which I have not courage," the Hungarian replied proudly. "What is it?"

"Are you courageous enough to hold the card for me whilst I shoot?" the beautiful Messalina said mockingly.

Without replying, he took the five of hearts, held at one corner and said:

"Cut the middle heart out, if you can."

She carelessly lit a cigarette aimed and fired.

"Capital," the colonel exclaimed, looking at the card. "Your bullet has turned the five into a four."

"Forgive me," the beautiful, frivolous woman cried, ashamed at her adorer's coolness, and threw her arms round his neck.

"Will you not shoot again?" he asked, with a sly smile.

"No, no," she whispered, burying her face on his breast.

The heart of the fickle woman now belonged altogether to the brave, handsome officer, but yet she hesitated to bring her connection with the other to an end. Whilst she was at her country-house in Baden, and also when she returned to Vienna in the autumn, she managed it so, that her lovers never met, and did not even suspect each other's existence. Whether it was the striking energetic manliness and artistic irritability, which the hussar and Maximilian offered her, and who both of them attracted her equally, whether it was a whim or whether it was a weakness, at any rate she accepted the homage of both, and made both of them happy.

One evening, when the Colonel was away on duty at some distance from Vienna, Baroness Amelia again received the young artist, so that she might talk about the last exhibition, new plays and new books with him, until at last she lavished all the raptures of love on him. Suddenly, however, the curtain over the door rustled unexpectedly, and the handsome hussar came into the small room, and remained standing as if he were turned to stone, at the sight which the group offered him, and which there was no mistaking.

The Baroness uttered a scream, and tried to cover the disorder of her dress as well as she could, whilst the two men stood opposite each other for a moment, exchanging hostile looks. Although there could not possibly be any greater contrast between the pale artist, with his long, light curls, and wrapped in a kind of long, black gown, and the vigorous hussar in tight, white breeches, black boots, and his short, light blue hussar jacket, trimmed with sable and covered with gold lace and holding his riding-whip in his hand, yet each of them immediately recognized a rival in the other.

"Only no scandal if you please," said the Baroness, who was the first to recover her composure.

"Calm yourself, Baroness," the colonel replied. "I think I have already given you sufficient proof of my coolness."

Then he turned to the young artist with haughty composure:

"I think, sir, that you will see that there is one too many here."

"I understand what you mean," Maximilian stammered; "you want your revenge; to fight a duel with me, but I have no idea how to handle any weapon. However, you are of course at liberty to murder me."

"What an idea! Who is thinking of murder?" the hussar replied. "If you do not understand how to use a sword or a pistol, there is nothing else left for us but a so-called American duel."

"What?" Maximilian said with difficulty, and growing white to his lips.

"We will draw lots," the colonel replied, "and whoever loses, will give his word of honour to commit suicide within twenty-four hours."

"That is quite correct," the young painter stammered.

"So your word of honour against mine," the colonel said, giving him his hand, and Maximillian slowly put his hand into that of his rival.

"Now I must beg for a pack of cards, Baroness."

She put one on the table.

"Will you be kind enough to shuffle them."

She did so, and then handed the pack to the young artist, for him to cut.

"Now let us each draw a card," the colonel continued; "red means life, black—death."

The Baroness handed the cards to the hussar, first, and then to the artist. There was a short pause, full of painful suspense; then the colonel calmly threw his card onto the table, and said: "Red."

"Black," the young artist said in a horrified voice; the piece of cardboard dropped from his hand, and fell on the ground at the feet of the Baroness, who picked it up and looked at it in curiosity.

"The queen of clubs," she said coldly, and the colonel looked at his watch and said:

"It is nine o'clock; you will have to keep your word of honour by this time tomorrow."

"Good heavens! This is too terrible," the young painter said, covering his pale face with both his hands. He was trembling all over with mortal terror and she seemed to have the scene on the Calvarienberg before her eyes again, and she felt inclined to spurn the wretched coward from her door.

"Must I really kill myself?" Maximilian began, looking at the colonel with the eyes of a madman.

"Will it not be enough for you if I renounce all my rights over Baroness Amelia?"

"No," the colonel replied; "this woman, whom I used to love, has betrayed me with you, and I mean to have satisfaction for it."

"I implore you to grant me my life, Colonel," Maximilian said.

"That is not the manner in which to beg for mercy," his rival replied, struck by a sudden thought. "Kneel down."

The young artist, who was only intent on saving his life, knelt down before his opponent, and begged for mercy, whilst the Baroness laughed contemptuously.

"Yes, I will grant you your life, but first of all I shall chastise you as you deserve."

The young artist looked at his rival in astonishment, who loosened the gold cords of his pelisse, so as to be able to use his arms better, and then took up his riding whip.

"You are going to beat me!" he stammered.

"Yes, but not with this switch, which is intended for noble animals," the hussar replied. "Where is your dog whip, Baroness?" She gave it to him hastily, and the next moment, he sprang on his rival like a tiger, threw him on the ground, and beat him like a dog, until he whined for mercy; then he flung him outside the door, and gave him a kick to help him on his way.

"Oh! what a perfect man you are," the Baroness, exclaimed in ecstasy; "I should like to kiss you!'

"No, Amelia," the handsome hussar replied; "the story must not end in such an idyllic fashion. Now it is your turn to beg for mercy!"

"What are you going to do? Do you intend to kill me?" the beautiful Messalina cried, in an agony of fear.

But the colonel only laughed, and at the same time struck the traitress, who has thrown herself on her knees before him, and begged him to forgive her, across the face and then over the bare shoulders, with his riding whip. Her prayers were all in vain, however, for he left her with a mocking contemptuous laugh, and never went near her again.

THE LETAWITZA

IT was an unlucky day for the chase: two hazel-hens and a big vulture comprised the whole booty. "It is the fault of that confounded sorceress!" exclaimed the gamekeeper, taking off his hat, and wiping the large drops of perspiration on his forehead on the puffed sleeves of his shirt; then he handed me some brandy in a gourd, yellow and chubby as a Barbary ape.

At dawn we had, it is true, in starting out on our expedition, met a little old woman, all withered up, who was searching for mushrooms in the brushwood; and now evening was falling, and there was nothing left for us but to return to the house. The sun was setting, red and angry, behind the huge blocks of granite that like great crumbling towers overhang the grey, jagged sides of the Carpathian Mountains. Nothing else was to be seen, unless it were an old stunted trunk, which, stretching out from the rubbish over the slippery declivity, seemed to reach towards us its long, gnarled arms. It stood projected against the sky, with its bent back, its hanging *chevelure* and mossy beard, absolutely like our Jew; but it clings, firm and immovable, to the rock, as he also knows how to hold on energetically to whatever his thin bony hands have once seized.

We descended rapidly by a path draped with bilberries and rhododendrons, our dog panting painfully behind us, and passed under the green canopy of pines. The subdued noise of a distant waterfall accompanied us. The tall, green, feathery tree-tops, which shot up toward heaven with solemn majesty, began to mingle with the golden, rosy horizon, while from their slender trunks escaped their amber-coloured resinous juice. Red and purple berries, with the large forest flowers, made designs like a many-coloured embroidery upon the velvety moss which spread among the interlacing roots; and deep shadows fell from above upon the branches, like black drops between the motionless needles.

A few minutes longer, little clouds hovered in the west, bathing themselves in the rosy sea; then a line of purple extended along the horizon. Above the ground the soft, tremulous air was filled with innumerable little flies transparent as spun glass, and vapours, that might have been taken for white veils of an impalpable material, ascended with brilliant reflections from the tranquil valley, already plunged in night. The bushes, the trees, the mountains, seemed to shoot up in the golden atmosphere and lose themselves in the infinite, while their shadows stretched out ever farther. In the west, a star glittered above the pines, which stood erect against the sky like black swords, or like iron pickets around a park. The songs of birds had ceased. Here and there, only, a whistling sound pierced the forest, and some affrighted animal fled among the branches.

The pearly sky had become blue, and gradually darkened. The shadows closed around, and at last were inextricably mingled with the impenetrable mass of slowly thickening gloom. Having, at this moment, reached the foot of the wooded hill, we followed a narrow path which wound around between common pastures and potato-fields. Suddenly the dark space between two rocks towards the west was illuminated, and began to flame as if some village were on fire; then, after a moment, the moon unmasked her golden disk, suspended majestically in the obscurity of the heavens, and diffused over the country her mild, consoling light. A current of cool air passed over the stalks, the grasses, the leaves of the trees, and the dismal summits of the pine forest; everything began to swarm, to flutter, to murmur. Far in advance of us the lights of a village gleamed like glow-worms lying in the grass, and overhead the immense vault was strewn with innumerable stars, like the bivouac fires of a grand army. The moonlight lay along the branches like threads of silver, and all the hills, all the ravines, were swimming in this magical reverberating light, which produces in us at the same time such calm and such melancholy.

As we reached a little cluster of birches, a flashing rocket traversed the sky and disappeared in space. The gamekeeper crossed himself, and stopped short. "Too late, the evil has come," said he.

"What evil?"

"Didn't you see the star shoot?"

"Certainly."

"It will be transformed into a *letawitza*."

"How is that?"

"In every shooting star there lives a demon which falls upon the earth," replied the gamekeeper in a troubled voice. "If at the instant when one perceives it he recites a certain formula, the witchcraft is conjured away, but if the star touches the earth it takes the form of a woman of great beauty, with long blonde hair which flows and glistens like stars. This beautiful creature is gifted with a strange power over every human soul. She draws young persons to her in the golden network falling over her white shoulders. At night, when all sleep, she bends over them and embraces them,—embraces them pitilessly, until they fall dead."

The gamekeeper had not finished his recital when we seemed to hear afar off, as it were, a deep sigh. This wail burst upon the solemn silence which hung over this sombre copse in the midst of the birches with their perpetually agitated leaves, whose trunks, white as the dead in their winding-sheets, seemed to stand upright around us, mute, and pointing their fingers at us.

"What was that?" I asked.

"An undine, or possibly a *roussalka*; perhaps even the *letawitza*."

"I thought it was a bittern, rather."

"Well, call it so, it is a bittern," returned the gamekeeper with a sort of pity. "In any case we'd better continue our course."

We had taken but a few steps when a flame about the height of a man rose up beside us in a thicket of dwarf alders. It waved to us, bowed down to the earth, and then began to leap before us as if it had a mind to accompany us."

"A will-o'-the wisp!"

"The lord grant it may only be a will-o'-the wisp!" said the gamekeeper in a low tone; "but I'm afraid the day will not end well."

"Are there some marshes near here?"

"Yes, certainly. There is even a pond. It must be off here to our right."

Reaching the end of our path, we saw, through the thicket, what seemed a mirror reflecting the light of tapers. I went towards it.

"You are not going to expose your soul to such danger?" groaned the gamekeeper.

Without replying to him, I parted the branches and opened for myself a way to the edge of the pool. The will-o'-the wisp had disappeared, but the bittern renewed its melancholy cry. The gamekeeper recited his conjuration aloud. We stood upon the border of a large sheet of water, which, lighted by the moon, stretched out at our feet. Some alder-bushes, erect among the brambles, were mirrored mysteriously in the lake. Their roots bathed in it, their long branches trailed in it like floating hair. It was both sad and impressive.

Suddenly, a childish laughter burst forth, pure, clear, and mocking like the tinkling of a silver bell. Bubbles rose to the surface of the water. Luminous little waves agitated it, a thousand sparkles played about each other on the pool, and, in the midst of a whirl of foam, we saw come forth a young woman of strange beauty. Her thick blonde hair, overflowing her marble shoulders, diffused itself in a starry shower. She fixed upon us two large black eyes, radiant and full of mockery.

"God have mercy on my poor soul!" cried the gamekeeper. "Shut your eyes!" and he drew me along. "We must fly!" repeated he in a trembling voice, "fly! or it is all up with us."

A second burst of laughter, yet more Satanic than the first, resounded harshly in our ears.

I followed the gamekeeper. An unknown power, which I could not explain to myself, gave me wings. We traversed, always running, thickets, marshes, meadows. Arrived at the orchard, we arrested our course to take a breath.

"You are nothing but an ass!" said I, by way of conclusion.

"Much better be an ass than be damned."

"Fly before a pretty woman!"

"Ah, yes! she was pretty," returned the gamekeeper; "but she does not belong to the earth. It is the *letawitza*, the shooting star which has assumed a human form. You did not, then, observe her hair? Wouldn't you have called it a trail of stars floating on the surface of the water?"

"I am going back down there! I must see that woman."

"Are you, then, possessed by a devil?" said the gamekeeper, petrified; "if you laid before me a hundred ducats, if you offered me the whole world, I would not stir an inch from here."

"But, if I offered you a glass of brandy, would you accompany me?"

"Brandy? what brandy? not rye brandy, I hope."

"Some *slivowitz*, if you like."

The good man heaved a sigh, whistled to his dog, and slowly directed his course towards the pond. I followed in his path, several steps to the rear. A gold-coloured will-o'-the-wisp accompanied us, as if to lighten our way. While we followed the fantastic flamelet, which passed sometimes to the right, sometimes to the left, whirling under the branches, lengthening itself out on the moss like a snake, or hovering in the air above us, we found ourselves up to the knees in the swamp.

The moon was hidden behind a cloud, as if she were in a conspiracy with the elves to mystify us. The alders, until now motionless and silent, rocked with a dull, rustling sound. The jarring cry of the bittern struck harshly on the ear. Then the water plashed almost over us. It was the dog, which plunged in and with sturdy barks announced to us that we had reached the end. I leaped precipitately over the thick branches, and found myself on the edge of the lake, where the moon, smiling and disentangled from her veils, seemed to contemplate its peaceful face.

The woman with golden hair had disappeared. We saw her neither in the waves where just before she had glittered like a star, nor on the shore, where her white form had stood in relief like a luminary against the blackness of the alders. Now all reposed in mournful silence: not a ripple upon the water, not a breath among the leaves. And in the middle of the pool rose majestically towards heaven a pale water-lily, mounting upward like a white flame.

The gamekeeper drew a long breath.

"God has protected us," murmured he, "but let no one say now that it was not the *letawitza*."

THE BEAUTIFUL VIVANDIÈRE

IT was in the evening during the last war, after a brilliant victory for German arms, when the thunder of the cannons had ceased, and the tired soldiers had thrown themselves down on the blood-stained earth, and their watch-fires were flaring all round. One corps had covered itself with glory above all others, and had carried the most important positions by assault, but had also suffered the severest losses. Its commander, a brave Prince, belonging to a German house, had set a splendid example at the head of his soldiers, and now he was riding slowly through their ranks, in order to reward the brave fellows with hearty words, to condole with the wounded, and here and there to regret one or another of them, with whom he had been personally acquainted. At last he arrived at the bivouac of a battalion of riflemen, tired, hungry and thirsty, and so he dismounted and asked for a glass of wine. The *vivandière* was immediately sent for and, and came with her little cask, and handed the illustrious general the wine with a saucy smile. That moment decided the future of both of them.

After the Prince had emptied his glass, he remained talking for some time with the pretty, buxom girl, who had greatly taken his fancy, and then quite unceremoniously, in spite of the fact that his soldiers were all about them, he began to make love to her. The *vivandière* was, in the fullest sense of the word, what might be called a camp-beauty; tall, with a full bust, rounded arms, a well-shaped head and finely chiselled features, large, bright, black eyes, and an abundance of black hair. She was one of those women who not only send common soldiers and camp followers into raptures, but one who would please any man; except that a predominant look of effrontery on her face, warned the prudent, experienced man of the world, and deterred him from carrying matters to any length. Now our Prince was neither imprudent nor inexperienced, but merely terribly-surfeited with women, and so perhaps that very thing which would have kept any other refined man off, attracted him to the buxom wench. The scene by the camp-fire ended in the general putting his arm round her waist, and kissing her heartily on her red lips, to which she replied, first, by a shameless laugh, and then, by a vigorous cuff.

For a moment, the Prince was quite dumbfounded, then he also laughed, and made his Adjudant take down her name in his notebook.

That amusing incident was the subject of much talk in the army the next day, and then it appeared to be forgotten, and the pretty *vivandière* with it. Peace was concluded, and the troops returned to their different garrisons whilst the Prince received the command of a large district. Not long after he had settled down in the province, a lady came to reside there, who attracted all eyes by her rich and extravagant dress and her rather bold demeanour, and in military circles she was said to be the Prince's mistress. Before long a non-commissioned officer recognized her as the former pretty *vivandière*, who had taken the Prince's heart by storm through the resolute use of her strong little hand. The pretty wench, who had formerly served Madame Venus, that beautiful she-devil, in the Capital, as her high priestess, and who then had gone through thick and thin with soldiers and their horses, and who had slept, like them, on the bloodstained earth, now lived like a princess, as the female commander of a general in command, and spent the life of a Turkish Sultana. As soon as she had discovered that it was just the coarseness of her manners, and above all her incredible shamelessness, which had the greatest charm for this Prince, who was so worn out with pleasure, and so spoilt and flattered by everybody, she profited recklessly by her advantages, and caused him a thousand petty embarrassments.

At the same time, she formed a bold plan for attaching her princely lover to her altogether, and she carried it out with wonderful cleverness and revolting hypocrisy. After the lapse of about half a year, and when she felt quite secure of her power over the Prince, she, one evening, in the midst of the caresses of a lover's meeting, told him that she was pregnant by him, which was a lie, however. And that was not all. The beautiful *vivandière* did not hesitate for a moment to add the lowest, most arrant deceit to the lie.

Then began a comedy, which was at the same time both laughable and sad, and the former soldiers' *Venus* acted it so well, that not only her lover, the Prince, but everybody, even her immediate attendants, were taken in. He was in a state of the highest bliss, and already began to form all kinds of plans for his son's future, for he never doubted for a moment that it would not be a son, and luckily the beautiful *vivandière* was in the position be able to fulfil his warmest wish.

As she knew perfectly well that the Prince was tied to the Capital of the province by his military duties, she told him a month before her pretended confinement, that she would await the event in a small town some distance off, in order to escape the talk of the malicious tongues, and the Prince was infatuated enough not to see through her design, and weak enough to agree to her proposal. Thereupon she went to her parents, who lived in a small town in a remote part of Hungary, so as to be perfectly safe from any visit of her lover at the decisive moment, but his passion and his tenderness for the beautiful *vivandière* were so great, that he went after her a few days before the catastrophe, and she would have been lost, if he had not, to his own detriment, informed her of his impending arrival, by telegram.

Then it was a case for prompt action. That female imposter formally, and in a regular manner, bought the newly born child of a peasant woman in the neighbourhood for a considerable sum, under the pretext that she wished to adopt a newly born infant and bring it up as her own, as she had no children, and when the Prince arrived, the beautiful *vivandière* was in bed, and in a cradle by her side, was a pretty healthy boy

The joy of the illustrious father has boundless. There was a splendid christening; mother, child and all their relations received the most lavish and princely gifts; her unexampled fraud had succeeded and the Prince was fettered forever to the vilest creature in the world, by indissoluble bonds.

The Prince returned first to the town, which was the headquarters of the military district which he commanded, and in a few weeks the woman whom he loved, and by whom he had been so shamelessly deceived, followed him. She, however, was not satisfied with the result, great as it was. She went on acting the comedy with unexampled audacity, made her appearance in public in places of fashionable resort amongst the ladies of the aristocracy, and had the child carried behind her, by a spruce Hungarian nurse. It was in vain that the Prince begged her not to do so; and for a long time there had been no question of commanding, on his part. The more he represented to her that she was compromising him, the more recklessly she did it, as she wished to expose him to his subjects, to his courtiers and to the world in general, in order to force him to marry her. But just before playing her last card, she also determined to secure her future against all eventualities.

One evening she told him that painful as it might be to her, she felt herself obliged to sever her connection with him, as she owed that much to her child. A Russian nobleman, who was madly in love with her had offered his hand, his name and a liberal marriage settlement, which would secure the full possession of his great fortune, to her and of her child.

The Prince was startled, he felt that his whole life was already so interwoven with that of the bold self-interested woman, that he could not grasp the mere idea of losing her. He threw himself at the imposter's feet and implored her not to leave him; she might make any conditions she pleased. She, therefore, demanded 20,000 florins for herself, and the same amount for the child, within a fortnight's time, and she made him give her a solemn, written promise, that he would marry her as soon as he had obtained the consent of his ministers. Even she had not expected such a rapid and complete triumph.

Then she burst all bounds, and her life became as unbridled as Messalina's was. She received her favourites openly and shamelessly, at her own house, for she knew that the torments of jealousy would only stimulate her satisfied lover; and these were not young dandified officers, or enthusiastic students, but herculean, non-commissioned officers, circus-riders and lion-tamers, and in company with them and common women she celebrated noisy orgies, which disturbed the nightly repose of the neighbourhood. Once, when the noise became too outrageous, the Prince suddenly came out of her bedroom in his dressing-gown, and told them that they had had too much wine, and must be quiet. But she pushed him out of the room, and locked him in, so as to be secure from any further interruption on his part.

Similar scenes were of almost daily occurrence; they alarmed the Court and the townspeople, lowered the Prince in the eyes of his soldiers, and at last drew everybody's attention to their connections. At first he received a quiet hint from higher quarters, not to allow the affair to attract too much attention and the Prince told his mistress this, and in his shy way, joined in the wishes of his family. But this had exactly the opposite effect, and all the furies seemed to have been let loose suddenly in the breast of the beautiful *vivandière*.

She began to dress in the most striking manner, and to behave even more strikingly. Hitherto, she had been satisfied with rousing the anger of the aristocratic ladies on the fashionable promenade; but now she began to ride, and she always rode in the most eccentric costume, just where the cream of society was, and she bought carriages and horses, and she handled the reigns as well as any noble Amazon herself. She rented a box on the first tier at the theatre, and blazing with diamonds appeared in it every evening to the disgust of everybody; kept her opera glasses fixed incessantly on the Prince, and when she was in a good temper, she even nodded at him, without caring the least what impression it might make on the spectators, and without troubling herself about the angry folds in the forehead of her princely lover.

During the Carnival, as the Prince was not able to procure her the *entreé* to the balls of the nobility, she frequented the public masked balls, and behaved so abdominally there, whether disguised as a *Bayadère* or unmasked, that the commissary of police more than once felt inclined to remove her, and was each time only prevented from doing so through the intervention of the town major.

Another, and much stronger knit, was received from high quarters, but this also had no effect; but just at the moment when the beautiful *vivandière* was mocking and defying the whole Court and city with incredible insolence, the catastrophe occurred, which was her ruin.

At the time when she asked for, and received, the 40,000 florins, the Prince had raised part of the monies from usurers at enormous interest, and when the time for repayment came, he was not in a position to satisfy his creditors' claims, so they applied to the King.

Then the Court interfered energetically, and all the more so, because his creditors made their claims almost at the same time that the Prince asked for permission to marry the *vivandière* morganatically. The Prince was ordered to relinquish his command and to leave the town where he was quartered within twenty-four hours, and he was transferred to the Capital, where he could be carefully watched.

At the same time, the police arrested his mistress by the King's orders, and she was sent out to the country; whereupon she returned to her parents in Hungary. And now that her star had set, a traitress was found in her own family who, seduced by the prospect of a handsome reward, accused the beautiful *vivandière* of the most abominable fraud.

A secret investigation was ordered, from which it was proved that the Prince's mistress had acted the most abominable part in pretending that she had had

a child, that the child was not hers, but belonged to
a peasant woman, and that she had made use of all
these means in order to obtain those sums from the
Prince, which were the cause of all his present embarrassment. The sentence which the beautiful *vivandière*
received, was a tolerably severe one, and she was sent
to gaol for a lengthened period.

The Prince, however, was by no means cured
when his mistress's frauds were thus unmasked; he
was only driven to despair through her loss, and she
had scarcely been set at liberty, when he was again
lying at her feet.

MARCELLA

RETURNING home after an absence of ten years, I chanced to meet one of the friends of my youth, Count Alexander Kossarof, who immediately insisted on my becoming his guest for the hunting season.

The count was about twenty-eight years of age, tall, well-formed with muscles of steel and an imposing stature. His face, with its serve features, grave, deep-set eyes, fair and somewhat auburn hair and pointed beard, was one of the true Little Russian type.

Something of the untamed Cossack there was in this temper, and his manner was abrupt, almost savage at times. If he wished to gather a plum, for instance, he broke off branch and all. In short, he was one of those men whose will is stronger than nature or destiny, and although endowed with rare alacerity and great sensibility, he was not governed by his imagination.

He was said, moreover, to disdain women, to be a misogynist. One day, as we were taking tea together after a day's shooting, having changed our boots and wet garments, I questioned him on this subject. He smiled.

"It is very natural," he replied. "I have no time. Instead of gambling or paying court to some pretty woman, I am working like a peasant to bring back my ruined estate into something like order; instead of contracting new debts, I am trying to pay off my father's old ones. But in reality I am so far from disdaining the fair sex that I am thinking seriously of marrying."

"You!"

"Yes, I. So long as I have no housekeeper here, there will be no order in the place."

"Very well; but where will you find what you need?"

"I wish to find her," he replied, calmly, "and I shall. But I do not intend to marry what is called a woman of the world. There are many such, and I have had my warning. I have visited Italy, Spain, France, England and the east, and I have kept my eyes open. I have loved, and I have been loved. But at last I was seized by a contempt for the world and a longing for the Arcadian simplicity of my own country home. One night, seated at the feet of the lady, whom I thought I admired, upon the terrace of her villa, near the Bosporus, beneath a star-lit sky, while Lady Isabel watched the waves and a slave fanned her burning cheeks, there flashed across my mind—I know not why—an old story of my nurse's. Doubtless you know it—'The Fairy Tale of Happiness?'"

"I forgot it."

"Then I will repeat it to explain myself. Once upon a time, three brothers lived in a great dark forest, not far from the blue sea. They lived there alone.

One day the eldest said: 'Beyond the forest there is a high mountain, and beyond the mountain there is a great and fertile land.' The second brother said: 'Beyond the forest there is also the blue sea, and beyond that sea are rich cities.' And the third brother said: 'Shall we find there trees like those in our forest or birds which sing as sweetly as ours?' But the eldest said: 'Let us depart and seek our fortune.' And the second said: 'Yes, let us go forth to seek our fortune.' But the third brother said nothing. Then, they saddled their proud black horses and seized their sharp pointed lances, and all three went in search of their fortune. The eldest passed the mountains and entered the fertile land—the second crossed the blue sea in a ship to visit the great cities, and they sought for happiness everywhere, but found it not. The youngest alone did not go far, only to the edge of the forest. There his heart swelled within him, and he said to his black steed: 'We shall do better to return home to our house in the forest'—and he turned back. Then the branches murmured gently and bent down before him, and the birds followed him, singing till the whole forest seemed to echo: 'Thou didst well to return.' And when he stopped before his house there he saw a fair maiden with golden hair, who sat within the threshold, spinning, while beside her the cat purred in the sunshine. 'Who art thou?' She looked at him with gentle smiling eyes, and answered: 'I am your happiness.'"

"Your legend is very pretty," I exclaimed.

"I remembered it in time," he said. "My heart was weary for home. I had no rest until I returned. There

I found many changes. My mother was dead. The estate was in a bad condition. My father resigned the reins of government to me. I buried myself here, and saw no one—not even my relatives or neighbours—not even my old nurse, who lives on the other side of the forest—while I was endeavouring to restore the property. Things were looking somewhat better, when my father died, about six months ago. Since I have been alone with old Hendrik, but I shall not always be alone! Every time I come home in the evening, dusty and heated, it seems to me that I shall find the maiden with the golden locks upon my threshold, but there is never anyone here, save the old, blind and lame dog, who wags his tail at the sound of my footsteps. But it is late, and you seem sleepy. Good night, my friend."

We separated for the night. When I met him at breakfast—"Do you know," he said, "last night I dreamed with my eyes open? I saw my old nurse seated near my couch, and telling me her legend, while at her feet there sat my happiness—a young and lovely woman. What surprised me was that her hair was not golden but chestnut. She had a spindle in her hands and spun. I leaned on my elbow to see her better, when she lifted her eyes to mine, and by her eyes I knew her."

"Yes, her eyes are blue," said the old servant, quietly as he stood behind the count with his napkin over his arm.

"What in the world are you talking about? Who has blue eyes?"

"Why—Marcella."

"And who is Marcella?" asked the count, in stupefaction.

"Old Hainia's granddaughter, and the daughter of Nikita Tchornochenko, who lives at Zolobad," answered old Hendrik, not understanding the impression he had produced.

"My nurse has a granddaughter!" exclaimed the count, "with chestnut hair?"

"And blue eyes. Yes, sir," said Hendrik.

"You know her?"

"She is said to be a very good and beautiful girl, and not at all stupid."

The count appeared to be musing deeply. "It is strange," he murmured. "One of these days I must go to see the old woman."

We had lost ourselves in the impenetrable forest. The sun was already low; his rays shone between the reddening trunks which surrounded us on all sides.

"I should be angry," said the count, "if it were not my own fault. It is your place to reproach me."

"I don't mind," I answered, laughing. "We are very well off as it is," and I sat down on a freshly cut tree stump.

"It would be the wisest plan," rejoined my friend, "to sit down and wait, whilst we call out now and then for assistance. Some hunter, woodcutter or mushroom gatherer may pass." He put his hands before his mouth and cried: "Holloa! Holloa!"

"Holloa!" answered the forest.

We then called together but the echo alone replied. Tired at last, we lay down on the dry leaves and divided our last bottle and the remnants of a cold lunch. An hour thus passed. Twilight advanced. "Come," said the count, "let us try our luck once more."

Hardly had he spoken when the distant notes of a soft, deep voice—that of a woman singing—fell on our ears. The song was wild and strange—the voice as peculiar.

"Do you know that air?" asked the count.

"Yes," I answered, "it is the song of the witches."

It was possible now for us to hear the words as the singer grew nearer.

> "Go not near the spinners,
> At midnight alone;
> For there in the darkness
> Their ill-deeds are sown:
> If you see the flames rising,
> Beware of the hour!
> The witch has your heart-strings"

"Holloa! Holloa!" I cried.

"Oho, the witch!" cried the count. "Where are you?"

The voice was now close upon us, as she repeated the last couplet. Through the trees we saw the slender figure of young peasant girl approaching us.

"What do you wish?" she asked in her soft, deep voice, stopping a few steps from us and looking at us in an almost forbidding manner.

"We are lost," I said.

"Do not go in the woods if you do not know the paths," she returned in a tone of rebuke.

I was silent and turned to the count for aid. He was quietly contemplating the young girl, who stood before us in a haughty attitude, as if she felt the royalty of her maidenhood. The same dazzling purity shone in the folds of her snowy bodice, as in her face and features. She was beautiful but her beauty was proud and cold. Though tall and willowy, her figure was full and rounded. The coquettish costume of our peasant women, the full skirt and soft bodices of blue cloth, with a puffed white chemisette, singularly became her. Her bare neck and arms were brown. The perfect oval of her face was burned by the sun, her lips were a deep red and her silky chestnut hair fell in soft curls around a high forehead and was confined in two heavy braids tied with crimson ribbon. Her large blue eyes looked still larger and deeper beneath her dark lashes.

"The type of the Fornarina!" said the count to me in French, without raising her eyes from her face.

The young girl understood that he was speaking of her. She knitted her brows angrily, and exclaimed: "What do you want? Why do you talk to each other?"

"We have lost our road," said the count. "Will you show it to us?"

"To Lesno."

"Well—follow me then."

She walked on, we following.

"What is your name?" asked the count at the end of a few moments.

She did not answer.

"I asked you your name," he repeated in a slightly imperative tone.

"Have I asked you yours?" she retorted coldly.

"This little witch is not wanting in logic," murmured the count. "Where did you get those eyes?" he continued after a pause.

Instead of replying she walked on more quickly. The count joined her and walked at her side "I like you," he said again. She looked at him without a word, but her glance spoke volumes.

"Come with me," persisted my friend, in a spirit of badinage. "I am rich. You shall live in my chateau and wear silk and satin. You shall have jewels and furs and ride out in a carriage drawn by four snow-white horses."

The poor girl's face was crimson. "Why do you insult me?" she exclaimed, and her voice broke into a sob.

"I did not intend to insult you", returned the count.

"By what right do you dare to speak to me?' she went on "God has made all men alike. You may be a noble, but before Him I am as good as you. Why do you insult me?"

"But you can understand it," said the count. "You are a pretty girl and please me. What should I say? Do you imagine, for instance, that I ought to ask you to marry me?"

"I should not think of such a thing," she exclaimed, bursting into a peal of laughter. "How could we live together? Like a horse and a cat harnessed to the same cart. But if you mean that I am not good enough to be your wife, I can tell you that I am too good to be anything else."

"You are a good girl," said the count, warmly, "I like you even better now. Give me your hand"

She hesitated.

"Give me your hand," he repeated, authoritatively, and she obeyed. They walked side by side till we left the forest. It was dark and the stars had come out.

"Here is the road," said the young girl, pointing. "Keep to the right and you cannot miss it."

She gathered a flower as she stood still beside us.

"Where do you live?" asked the count. No answer.

"Where can I see you again?" persisted my friend.

"Why do you wish to see me again?" she rejoined, casting an inscrutable glance at him.

"Well—no matter!" said the count. "I can easily find you. But now thank you and goodnight."

He held out his hand, and seeing that she kept hers hidden in the folds of her skirt, he seized upon it, and shook it heartily then took off his hat with a courteous bow, as he turned away to the road she had indicated.

"Goodnight!" she cried out after we had gone some distance, and set off running along the edge of the forest.

The count watched her vanish in the darkness. "She must be my wife," he murmured.

"How can that be?" I asked.

"I do not yet know that myself, but I feel that she is already mine: that she shall be my own."

The next day he came into my room and said in a low tone of voice: "Do you believe in second-sight?"

"I do not know. Why?"

"I believe in it. My mother was a seer; she foretold things that were to happen long after, and I too, have strange presentiments, which are generally realized."

"And what presentment was yours?"

"I told you I wished to marry," he said, "then I dreamed of my nurse, and at her feet my happiness in the form of a maiden with long chestnut hair and large blue eyes. That woman is the unknown of the forest and that unknown is—Marcella, my nurse's granddaughter—and, you shall see it, Marcella, will be my wife."

"Are you losing your mind? A peasant?"

"I am conscious of what I say, and I shall be happier with her than ever mortal before."

"So you are determined?"

"There is no determination about it. I see what must be. I have seen Marcella, not in her peasant dress, but in a robe of velvet and ermine, and she was surrounded by her children. This afternoon we will go to call on my nurse, and, you shall see, Marcella will be seated on the threshold spinning."

As we approached the farm of Nikita Tchornochenko, near the village of Zolobad, I could not help a certain feeling of expectancy. The wolf-dog was chained, and could only follow us with his eyes. The gate was open. In the yard stood a peasant's cart of willow and near it three brown and lean horses, one of them a colt. The wooden white-washed house, thatched with blackened straw stood before us, and on the threshold was seated a young girl spinning, at her side a white cat, who stretched itself in the sun and blinked its eyes as it saw us. The girl looked up and started. She was the unknown of the forest.

"You are Marcella?" said the count.

"What do you wish?" she replied.

"Is your grandmother at home?"

"Yes. Will you be good enough to walk in?"

We entered. In the centre of the large bare room was seated a little boy of eight, bare-headed, with an earthenware basin upon his head. A middle-aged man was clipping the boy's hair, guided by the outline of the platter.

"Where is my nurse, Hainia?" asked the count.

"Who wants me?" exclaimed a voice from the next room, and a tall old woman with snowy hair came in. Her eyes rested on the count. "Good heavens!" she stammered. "Is it possible? Is it, indeed, you, Sacha?"

The count's arms went around her neck, and the old woman, sobbing, covered his bronzed face with kisses.

"Sacha, my beloved child," she faltered. "How you have grown! Come in, all of you. Marcella, Nikita, Eva, come see my child Sacha!"

In a moment the room was full

"Here is my son-in-law, Nikita Tchornochenko," said the nurse. "Come and speak to the count."

"Your highness, I am glad to see you," spoke the peasant, somewhat embarrassed. "Where is Marcella? My second daughter," she explained as she approached. "Here is the eldest, Eva, and Bodak, her husband. They have already three children. And here are Liska and Vachkou, my own youngest," pointing

200

to a shy little girl, and to the boy, who still sat on his stool, with the earthenware bowl on his head, not daring to move.

The old woman, too happy for words, still smiled at her nursling, but finally, she led us into an inner room, where we took our seats on the bench near the large green stove, while Nikita and his daughter drew up the table. The nurse took Marcella's hand and placed her before the count.

"Look at her," she said, "a favoured child, like you were too. She is a good girl . . . eighteen years old, strong and straight as a young tree, and with the best of hearts. My child, if you were not a count, and she a peasant, what a wife she would be for you!"

"How you talk, grandmother!" interrupted Marcella, reddening up to her eyes as the count looked at her attentively.

"Well, there is no harm done," said the old woman. "Bring in the curds, butter, cheese and bread—also some fresh milk for the children."

Marcella, departing, soon returned with a great bowl of curds, followed by Liska, bearing a pat of butter and cheese, while Vachkou, free from his headdress, carried the loaf of black bread. Marcella's father handed us two wooden spoons, and the count took out his hunting knife to cut our bread and cheese.

They all watched us eat. The old peasant smoked his pipe. The grandmother sat with her hands folded. Marcella took up her spindle again, and Nikita's son-in-law, the old peasant, came in with a large bowl of milk for the children.

Eva sat down the baby she held, and it was joined by two other little ones from two to four, who, each with spoon in hand, sat around the bowl upon the earthen floor. They dipped their spoons in and supped the milk noisily. The sun through the windows threw little golden squares upon the floor; the cat slept near the stove, while the swallows of the eaves came and went through the open door.

The noise which the babies made was soon heard. Suddenly from beneath the stove there crept out a small serpent, followed by another, both in haste to reach the milk. I rose, thinking the children in danger.

"Do not disturb yourself," said the old nurse, "those are our household snakes. Their nest is under the stove, and as soon as they hear the spoons they will always come out. They eat with the little ones, and sometimes sleep in the cradle."

"These snakes are harmless," added the count, "the peasant's friend, and his children's playmates. You find them in many houses and they are said to bring good luck."

"It is true," said Nikita.

The two snakes dipped their slender tongues into the milk which they drank so eagerly, the children began to fear the disappearance of their supper. The eldest calmly raised his spoon and tapped the head of the serpent nearest him. The animal drew itself away slowly, looked around with its small bright eyes, and then, gliding behind the child, passed round to the side of the youngest of whom he seemed least afraid, and once more began to sup.

"An idyllic scene," remarked the count.

I felt, like himself, the pleasing influence of his domestic scene. A vision of what happiness might mean flittered across my mind. Marcella, seated a little apart, was spinning, and seemed not to notice us. As it was growing late, the count rose, embraced his old nurse, shook hands with the two peasants, then with Eva and Liska, kissed the children and then only did he approach Marcella.

"Farewell," said he.

"God grant you happiness!" she responded, tranquilly.

"May He keep you as you are!" replied the count, touching her forehead with his lips. "Good night!"

"Good night!" they all exclaimed in chorus.

We silently traversed the village towards the edge of the forest, where the count sat down and gazed at the straw-thatched roof under which Marcella was born, and where her calm and tranquil life had been spent. He was silent for some time, then he murmured:

"I love her!"

"Alexander!"

"How can I help it? It is fate."

"You, a man of the world! And at first sight!"

"Love is either born of the first glance exchanged by two beings or never."

He rose and half mechanically turned back towards the village whither I followed him. He paused before the hedge of the farm. The words of the song came to our ears: "Go not near the spinners!" and through the open window of the farm house by the blaze of the firelight we saw Marcella standing over a huge pot into which she was shredding vegetables.

Her beautiful face bore a sombre expression and she was muttering phrases, which sounded like an incantation. "And so it is," remarked the count. "A charm."

"And for whose benefit?"

He was silent. Marcella continued the song:

> "If you see the flames rising,
> Beware of the hour!
> The witch has your heart-strings!
> You bend to her power."

"And the poison is in your veins," added the count. "The end is tragic. The witch poisons him, in jealousy, I think. It is a warning. Go on with your incantation. The story shall end with you and me as in my nurse's tale. You are no witch, but the Happiness which awaits me on that threshold—and I shall be ready for it when the time comes."

※

Alexander after this went every evening to Zolad, and I left him alone with Marcella as much as possible. He showed no outward anxiety, went on with his affairs as usual and appeared gay and careless. He rarely spoke of Marcella; his love for her seemed quiet, even timid.

One day, so he informed me, having found that it was her birthday, he brought her a coral necklace.

"She refused it, not angrily, but sadly. 'Would you prefer something else?' I asked her. 'I like you very much, and am anxious to prove it. What can I do for you?' She hesitated for some moments, then—'Teach me!' she said, abruptly. 'Teach you what?' I asked, not understanding.

"She pointed up to the stars, which sparkled above us.

"'Tell me what they are! Who holds the sun and moon in their places? Why do we see the plants spring up only to fade? Why do animals come into this world only to die? And what is our destiny?' I looked at her, and the tears came into my eyes."

The count thus began his lessons with an attentive pupil. He taught her to read, write and cipher, avoiding all the wearisome routine. He told her of the heroes of history and the mysteries of nature. He also brought her books of Russian poetry and songs.

One day I found him poring over *Faust*.

"Do you intend publishing a commentary?" I asked him.

"No—I am translating."

"Let us see! In the Little Russian dialect, and in prose! Is it to be printed?"

"Heaven forbid! It is for Marcella's use."

"This is serious then? Do you think she profits much by your instruction?"

"I have never yet found a mind so eager for truth and light."

"And do you understand her yet?"

"I begin to. She is called obstinate, but she never contradicts you, and calmly goes her own way. She is thought to be haughty and proud, because she does not laugh and blush at every trifle, like most young girls. She looks at you boldly and frankly. She is thought to be taciturn, but she is a good listener, and never stupid. She laughs seldom, but there is the light of a hidden smile upon her countenance, In short, she resembles her father. Remember this. When you choose a wife, look first at her father—lastly her mother, and if possible, the other ancestors. Marcella's grandmother, mother and, above all, her father, come of a fine stock."

I noticed Marcella's manner to the count during his frequent visits to Zolobad. She loved him evidently, but she fought fiercely against her love. She appeared almost to dislike him, and was disagreeable, and even rough in her manner towards him.

On this occasion, she was seated outside the cottage door as we came up. She reddened at the sound of our steps, but did not turn round to look at us.

"Good day, Marcella!" said my friend.

"Ah, is it you again, count?" she exclaimed, with a rude laugh. "You have nothing to do at home, then, that you come here so often. Yet they say your house is not so well managed as it should be."

The count did not answer this speech, but walked in to see his nurse. Marcella followed us in and began getting her spinning materials together. The count laid the manuscript of his *Faust* on the table.

"Here is the most perfect poem in the world," he said, "which I have translated for you."

"You might have spared yourself the trouble," she cried. "I am only a peasant. I have not mind enough to understand it."

"It is not the mind which is wanting!" said the count, looking her full in the face. "But oftener the

206

goodwill. For some time you have been rude to me. You were not always so."

"Well! so I am now", exclaimed she with heat. "I am not a gentle maiden, not a fine lady. Why should not I be rude? No one has ever taught me good manners."

"Do not hide behind your ignorance," said the count calmly. "Am I not willing to give you lessons? But you do not care to learn. As you please! If you wish to remain ignorant, you may. I have enough to do."

The grandmother rose and signed to him to follow her. He beckoned to me, and I went out with them. Once some distance from the house, she spoke: "My child, it will be for the best for you to come here no more."

"Why?"

"Why—because———"

"Because Marcella does not like me?"

"No. Because Marcella loves you."

The count was silent. We returned to the cottage shortly. We could see Marcella seated before the manuscript poems which he had left on the table and reading it slowly to herself, tracing the words with her fingers. He called to her through the window. She started—pushing the book away and blushed.

"Do you not think we can read it better together?" said the count.

She did not try to meet his mocking glance. "If you will be a little patient with me," she stammered. "I do not know what has been the matter with me for some time!" And she burst into tears.

The next day was sultry. The sky was a dark purple—the swallows flew close to the ground—no birds sang in the motionless foliage. Storm was in the air. The reapers had all come in. Only Marcella remained outside. We saw her in her red skirt, rising and sinking amidst the corn, like a poppy waiving in the breeze. The count went off to bring her in, but the first heavy drops of the storm fell, and they had not returned.

"Go and see what is the matter, sir," begged the old peasant woman, who stood at the door, gazing from under her uplifted hand.

I crossed the orchard. Arriving at the hedge, I perceived that Marcella and the count were arguing vehemently, almost angrily. Marcella, with her head wrapped in a flame-coloured kerchief, looked like a gypsy or a demon. She held a scythe in her right hand, while the other was extended, as though to repulse the count. She seemed to threaten him, while he, though pale, was smiling.

I hastened to join them.

Marcella, still moving backward, found herself stopped by the hedge. She raised the scythe, and as he endeavoured to embrace her, she brought it down, almost involuntarily as it seemed, on his head.

The blood spurted forth, but in an instance he had snatched the scythe from her hand and threw it far from him. Then he caught her in his arms and pressed her to his heart in spite of the fast-flowing blood from his wound.

The next day he appeared with the bandage on his head, but seemed neither pale nor weak, though he had lost a great deal of blood.

"What must I do now?" he asked me, smiling mischievously.

"You ought to give up tormenting that poor girl."

"I am going to marry that poor girl, my friend," he replied.

That evening we went as usual to the cottage. Marcella sat pale and subdued, her large tearful eyes fixed on the group. The count, seated near her, read aloud the last act of *Faust*.

"What do you think of it?" he asked, as he finished reading, laying the manuscript in Marcella's lap.

"What does it matter what I think?" she returned, without raising her eyes.

"It matters very much to me. I beg of you, tell me your thoughts."

Suddenly she rose, and looked proudly full in his face.

"Be it so. I will tell you that"—her voice quivered. "Your Faust, who is so learned, and whom nothing can satisfy, seems to me a great idiot, and his conduct towards Marguerite that of a coward. Oh! do not laugh! I quite understand. Here is a man who would like to be a king, almost a god, and what does he do to prove his power? he crushes another poor soul—I cannot say what I mean——"

"I understand you," said the count. "You are quite right, but you are getting as angry as if I were Faust himself."

"I know not if you are like Faust," replied Marcella coldly. "For I know that I am no Gretchen to throw myself at your feet."

※

I was obliged to leave Zolobad very suddenly, and to return to Vienna. I wrote to Count Kossarof on my arrival but it was not until two weeks thereafter, that I received a reply. The count wrote:

Lerno, Oct. 17, 185*

My Dear Comrade:

You will doubtless like to know what has happened since your departure. I need not tell you that I have spent most of my evenings at Zolobad. Marcella has been silent, gentle, almost subdued, but I pretend to take no notice of the change.

Yesterday afternoon, this is what occurred. You doubtless remember the pet snakes. The sun was still quite high as I came near the cottage, and upon the broad stones by the door-step lay a serpent basking in the sunshine. You know that I am fond of animals. I stooped to stroke the reptile, when it reared itself suddenly, bit my hand, and then glided off through the grass. Marcella just then appeared at the door.

"I was caressing your serpent," said I, laughing, "when the wretch bit me."

"Bit you? What serpent?" said she.

"Why, that one yonder."

Her eyes followed the direction in which I pointed, then she uttered a cry.

"Jesu-Maria!" and springing towards me seized my arm and laid her lips to the wound.

"What are you doing?" I asked in some embarrassment.

She signed me to be silent. Suddenly I understood.

"That was a venomous reptile, then?" She bent her head. "And you are sucking the poison? Good heavens!" I cried, and attempting to withdraw my hand, but she still held it firmly, until she could safely withdraw her lips.

"But you?" I said in horror. "It is as much as your life is worth."

"For you I would willingly die!" The cry burst from her lips with vehemence that almost alarmed me, then she burst into tears.

"You shall live for me!" I exclaimed. "You do love me—you are my own!"

She fell on her knees, and wept.

"Yes, I love you! I cannot live without you. I am not worthy to be your wife— but I will be your servant, your slave. For you I would leave my father and my mother, the house where I was born and even my native land, if you wished it, my beloved master!"

"You are my own," I repeated, "and you shall be my wife!"

"That cannot be," she stammered. "A poor peasant—how is this possible?"

I raised her, deeply moved. She wept in my arms.

You should have seen how the old people received the news. Tchornochenko wiped his eyes on his sleeve, while tears rolled down into his grey moustaches, and mother Hainia exclaimed: "Can it be possible, my children, that I should live to see such a thing?"

The banns will be published at the village church of Zolobad, and the wedding takes place in three weeks!

ALEXANDER

✳

In the autumn of 186*, at the end of the disturbances in Poland, I again found myself at Lesno, on a visit to Count Kornarof and his wife.

The old manor-house was covered with ivy, which climbed over the balconies, and wrapped the turrets in its embrace; vines hung with reddening grapes clustered along the side of the terrace; and roses bloomed on the law. The sweet murmur of the wood-pigeons sounded from the depths of the par.

Alexander soon appeared on the terrace, and pressed me in his arms, while tears shone in his eyes.

212

He led me into a drawing-room, which was hung with crimson damask, and laid with Persian gold-embroidered carpets.

The count must now have been forty years old, but he seemed younger than ever. "Here is my wife," he said, as at the end of a few moments Marcella's light step was heard. She entered, extending both hands to me, which I kissed.

"You will stay with us," said Alexander.

"As a matter of course," said Marcella. "He *must* stay."

"No; I must go at once."

"And why, if you please?" she asked quickly.

"Because madam," I said, bowing and smiling, "to tell truth, you are too beautiful for me to trust myself in your presence."

She was indeed a magnificently handsome woman, uniting the sweetest simplicity with the ease of a *grande-dame*, and possessing the elevated mind and cultivated intellect that are so rarely found in a woman.

"And where are your children?" I inquired.

Marcella went out, and soon returned, surrounded by her four children, three fine boys, who all resembled her, Sacha, Constinine and Julian, then the little Olga, whose regular features and grave eyes were those of her father. They gave me their hands frankly and without awkward timidity.

We visited the estate, the Countess putting on a broad straw hat in order to accompany us, and I witnessed all the improvements which Alexander had made. Next we rode out over the fields and beheld the extensive system of irrigation, the stock farms, the woods and quarries, finally the farms, with the beet-sugar factories. Everywhere were tokens of prosperity, content and order. A benediction seemed to rest on all things.

We returned in time for dinner. On leaving the table Alexander proposed a game of billiards, in which I was sadly beaten by Marcella. The count and I strolled out on the terrace for a smoke, but the evening was cool and it gave me more pleasure to return to the small drawing-room, where a bright fire sparkled on the hearth, and tea awaited us.

The young bear-cubs, as the Count called them, climbed on our knees. Marcella came down in a dress of grey silk, and garnet velvet, lined and trimmed with wonderful sable fur. She poured out tea for us, offered us cigarettes, and then went to the piano.

"Well," said Alexander, after a pause, "what are you thinking of so deeply?"

"I am thinking," I said, "of happiness, and I have come to the conclusion that true happiness consists alone in the effort made to attain it. We live each in a world of our own, and see it bright or dull, according the prism through which we view it."

"My happiness has lasted twelve years," said the Count. "Instead of passing our honeymoon in making love to each other, we have studied and worked together." He glanced towards a portrait of Marcella, which hung near us.

"I think," said I, "that you are still in love with your wife!"

"Of course I am!" he answered, "and every day I find in her some new charms. A woman never grows old for the one who loves her."

Little Ogla came in with her white cat; she carried a spindle, which she gave to her mother. Marcella left the piano, and came and sat by the fireside in a great arm-chair, where she began to spin, while the little girl watched the motion of her hand in absorbed attention. Soon the children all gathered around her chair. The cat jumped upon the velvet stool at her feet, and purred comfortably. The spindle danced, the cricket chirped in the chimney, and the fireside elves left their quiet nooks in the hearth corner to frolic invisibly around the fair spinner, and to sportively tangle the threads of her spinning.

"Look," said Alexander, as we gazed silently at the group, "here is my fairy tale realised. She is no longer the witch who played with my heart strings. Do you not recognise 'my happiness with the golden hair?'"

A PARTIAL LIST OF SNUGGLY BOOKS

MAY ARMAND BLANC *The Last Rendezvous*
G. ALBERT AURIER *Elsewhere and Other Stories*
CHARLES BARBARA *My Lunatic Asylum*
S. HENRY BERTHOUD *Misanthropic Tales*
LÉON BLOY *The Desperate Man*
LÉON BLOY *The Tarantulas' Parlor and Other Unkind Tales*
ÉLÉMIR BOURGES *The Twilight of the Gods*
CYRIEL BUYSSE *The Aunts*
JAMES CHAMPAGNE *Harlem Smoke*
FÉLICIEN CHAMPSAUR *The Latin Orgy*
BRENDAN CONNELL *Unofficial History of Pi Wei*
BRENDAN CONNELL *Metrophilias*
RAFAELA CONTRERAS *The Turquoise Ring and Other Stories*
ADOLFO COUVE *When I Think of My Missing Head*
QUENTIN S. CRISP *Aiaigasa*
LUCIE DELARUE-MARDRUS *The Last Siren and Other Stories*
LADY DILKE *The Outcast Spirit and Other Stories*
CATHERINE DOUSTEYSSIER-KHOZE
    The Beauty of the Death Cap
ÉDOUARD DUJARDIN *Hauntings*
BERIT ELLINGSEN *Now We Can See the Moon*
ERCKMANN-CHATRIAN *A Malediction*
ALPHONSE ESQUIROS *The Enchanted Castle*
ENRIQUE GÓMEZ CARRILLO *Sentimental Stories*
DELPHI FABRICE *Flowers of Ether*
DELPHI FABRICE *The Red Spider*
BENJAMIN GASTINEAU *The Reign of Satan*
EDMOND AND JULES DE GONCOURT *Manette Salomon*
REMY DE GOURMONT *From a Faraway Land*
REMY DE GOURMONT *Morose Vignettes*
GUIDO GOZZANO *Alcina and Other Stories*
GUSTAVE GUICHES *The Modesty of Sodom*
EDWARD HERON-ALLEN *The Complete Shorter Fiction*
EDWARD HERON-ALLEN *Three Ghost-Written Novels*
RHYS HUGHES *Cloud Farming in Wales*
J.-K. HUYSMANS *The Crowds of Lourdes*
J.-K. HUYSMANS *Knapsacks*
COLIN INSOLE *Valerie and Other Stories*
JUSTIN ISIS *Pleasant Tales II*